not so runaway bride

THE BRIDES OF SUNFLOWER FALLS

KATIE LILLIG

content notes

Dear Reader,

Thank you so much for your time in reading this book. I hope you enjoy it. I wanted to be sure to share some information about the book with you.

I never want anyone to have a bad reading experience with my books, so potential triggers I'm aware of in the book are listed below. I can't know everyone's triggers, so if I have missed anything that you think other readers need to know about, please feel free to email me at contentnotes@ katielillig.com and I will update this list every quarter on my website as needed.

- Child abuse, historical
- Death of parent, historical
- Emotional abuse, historical
- Gaslighting, historical
- Toxic relationship - parent/child
- Vomit, historical - mention only

one

DRIVING AROUND THE BEND INTO SUNFLOWER FALLS WAS LIKE THE opening of a movie, with Lake Ontario glistening in the early morning sunshine on the left and the town and woods behind it rolling up into hills on the right.

Libby Hartwell wasn't sure if she was in the middle of a rom-com or a horror movie. Considering the way the last twelve hours had gone, it could go either way. Though, the statement diamond engagement ring on her finger probably suggested a prestige drama.

The road into town provided glimpses of the lake between houses, and she saw several new construction sites mixed in with what looked to be lake houses that had seen generations of vacationers pass through them.

Her stomach rumbled, and she realized she needed food now. In the flurry of activity since she'd decided to come to Sunflower Falls, she hadn't thought to eat anything. She may still smell of a server's tray full of drinks from the bachelorette party, but she'd been stone-cold sober when she'd borrowed her best friend's car to drive the eight hours north to Sunflower Falls.

At least she'd been smart enough to take a brief nap at a rest stop about halfway up the state.

Two more minutes of driving and she spotted the Sunflower Diner with an impossibly kitsch sign on the edge of their parking lot. She waited as someone backed a huge SUV out of a parking spot and then pulled in.

She parked Greer's car in the empty spot and closed her eyes. The urge to sleep was just as strong as the need for food, but she could sleep later. And probably would sleep better once she got some food into her system.

Since this was a vacation town, hopefully there'd be a hotel or something she could rent for the night. She wasn't going back to New York City any time soon.

The early June air was clear and crisp at this time of day. Much different from the heat wave that had hit New York City. At least she wouldn't be a June bride who was sweating through her princess white gown. Maybe she could return it once she got home, since she'd only worn it for her fittings.

Inside the diner, conversations buzzed around the room, and servers performed complicated dances as they took and delivered orders. The one closest to her, a Black woman with her silvered hair pulled up in a bun, looked over and nodded at her. "I'll be with you in a moment."

"Thank you."

One of the other servers, a young white woman with her reddish blonde hair pulled back in a set of French braids, glanced over. "Just so you know, we're cash only."

Libby nodded. "Not a problem." Not a problem thanks to her best—well, only—friend Greer.

She took the time to examine the place she'd found herself in instead of preparing to walk down the aisle in... she glanced at the watch her father had given her as her twenty-first birthday present. Six hours. Six hours from now, she was to have been walking down the aisle to Herman Walker Clifford, the Fourth, better known to his friends as Cliff.

Or, better known to her father as Four. Personally, she'd never really settled on a name for him as they weren't exactly friends, but she also wasn't a partner at the firm their great-grandfathers had co-founded back in the day.

The server came over, interrupting the thoughts she'd been about to spiral down into. "How many?"

"Just me."

"Do you mind sitting at the counter?"

As the only open seating Libby had spotted was at the counter, and her stomach was about to pull an Alien move just to get some food, she was perfectly fine with that. "Not at all. Thank you."

The server grabbed a laminated menu and walked her over to the counter. There were a few seats open, but she pulled out the counter stool that was next to another woman with silvered hair, white this time. "Have a seat next to Mrs. Smith here. She'll take care of you with Bob."

Before Libby could say anything, the server headed back into the complicated dance of delivering hot food and coffee. Mrs. Smith turned in her seat and smiled at her. "Welcome. Are you visiting Sunflower Falls?"

Libby nodded. "I am."

"What brings you here? And alone? Is your spouse joining you later?"

"Spouse?" Libby winced as she heard the panic in her tone. She cleared her throat. "Um, no spouse."

Mrs. Smith's gaze took on a glint of curiosity. "Oh, interesting. Is there a fiancè or do you wear the ring to turn people off? That is a gorgeous ring, by the way. Whoever selected it did a magnificent job. Eye-catching, but elegant all at once."

Libby wondered who had selected the ring. It wasn't exactly her style, or Herman's for that matter.

"Thank you. No fiancè either. Not anymore."

Mrs. Smith reached over and patted her arm. "Their loss. Now, I need to know if you're vegetarian, vegan, or someone who just prefers not to eat meat."

"Uh, not any of those things?"

"Perfect. What you'll want to order is the Meat Lover's Skillet, as Nancy does a magnificent job with the home fries and hits the bacon at the perfect level of crispiness without being overly crisp. Such a hard line to maintain. I also recommend getting the eggs done over easy if you're not morally opposed to runny yolks. As for the side, I recommend the herbed bread with butter. Bob, despite being a disgruntled counter server, does amazing things with bread."

Disgruntled counter server Bob came up at that point and glared at Mrs. Smith. He grunted and turned to Libby. "Whatcha want?"

"Um..." She glanced down at the menu and was completely overwhelmed by all the choices. She pointed at Mrs. Smith. "What she said."

Bob glared. "The Smith Special. Coffee?"

She didn't care that the coffee wasn't made by some specialty cafe trained barista. She needed caffeine almost as much as she needed food. "Please."

Bob wrote her order on an old-fashioned paper pad as he walked away. He came back and deposited a thick white ceramic mug and saucer on the counter in front of her, and filled it to the brim with the black elixir of life. Not even room for any cream or sugar. She picked it up with both hands and carefully raised it to her mouth.

The scent hit her first. Rich and almost chocolatey. It

didn't smell burnt the way she expected diner coffee to be. She took a sip and hummed.

Mrs. Smith nodded. "They do have the best coffee around. Most of the regulars are here only for the coffee. We've converted quite a few tourists to drinking black coffee. At least while they're here."

Libby tuned her out and took another sip. She could feel the caffeine hit her system, even though she knew it couldn't be absorbed by the body that quickly.

She was going to need all the energy she could dredge up to accomplish what she'd come here for.

From the kitchen, a deep voice yelled out. "Counter order up."

She blinked when her order was plopped down in front of her. Bob had already moved down the counter to pour coffee for another person. She set her mug down and began digging in.

From the way she kept shoveling food into her mouth, she would have forgiven anyone for thinking she hadn't eaten in the last week. She had. But probably not as much as she should have, thanks to stress.

Wedding nerves got the best of the most committed people.

She just hadn't realized until last night how not committed she was.

"Was I right about the bread?"

Libby glanced at Mrs. Smith. She was sipping at her own mug of coffee, but she could tell the woman was smiling. "Yes. It's delicious." Bob was walking past. "Really delicious, Bob."

He grunted and continued on.

"He'll make sure your cup is always full the next time you're in here. What brings you to Sunflower Falls?"

"I received a letter from someone who knew my mother. They live here."

"Oh, really? An old roommate of hers?"

Libby shook her head. "I don't think so. Well, maybe, but that's part of why I'm here. I'd like to find out everything I can."

Mrs. Smith tilted her head. "Oh, dear. I'm sorry. When did you lose her?"

"I was a baby."

"And your father?"

"He rarely talks about her."

"Grief can be a vicious beast."

This time, Libby used the excuse of sipping from her coffee to deflect the need to respond. She had once believed her father had grieved her mother in his own way. But she also believed, now, that his reticence on discussing the woman who'd given her life was a way to control. Her mother or her, she wasn't sure.

But she had the opportunity to discover some of her mother's secrets and she'd do whatever was necessary to get those truths.

"Can you share who sent you this letter?"

"I'd prefer not to."

Mrs. Smith patted her arm. "Very wise, dear. If you run into any issues, however, come visit me. I have a little storefront on Lakefront Drive. Secrets and Whimsies. Drop in anytime."

"Thank you."

Libby wasn't sure what to do next, but she was done eating. She looked at what remained on her plate and couldn't bring herself to just leave it. As Bob passed by, she raised her hand and waved.

"What?"

"Can I get a to-go box for this, please?"

He grunted and reached under the counter. He handed her a cardboard container, and she emptied her plate into it, placing the last piece of bread on top.

"Thank you."

He grunted again and went to the kitchen window, coming back a minute later with her check and a bag. "You can pay Lydia up front."

"Thank you."

She turned to Mrs. Smith. "Thank you for the recommendation."

"You're welcome. Secrets and Whimsies. If the door's locked, just knock and I'll come open it if I'm in the store."

Libby got up and was making her way to the front. A man seated at a booth caught her eye, and he smiled. The luminescence of it had her step stutter for a moment, so she missed what caused the shouts coming from behind her.

But the next thing she knew, she was pushed from behind into the lap of the man seated at a table across from the grinning man in the booth.

He grunted and while the grinning man's smile had caused her to miss a step, the feel of the grunt reverberating through his body had her heart stuttering.

Libby tried to scramble out of his loose embrace, and every time she moved her hands, they met solid muscle. He was also trying to help her up, but they kept moving out of sync with each other, making the situation worse.

Warm laughter erupted from across the table. Libby looked over and saw a white woman about her own age wearing a worn logo t-shirt and her light brown hair pulled up in a messy bun. She wasn't wearing makeup, and her ears were filled with studs and small hoops.

"Melody, knock it off."

The man whose lap she currently occupied wrapped his

very well-muscled arm around both of hers and squeezed. "Hold still."

Unable to ignore his command, she froze.

"Good girl. I'm going to lift you up, so be ready to get your feet under you."

She nodded, and a moment later he moved, lifting both of them with ease. She felt the muscles of his thighs shift beneath her butt and had the extremely inappropriate thought—considering the circumstances—of what they might feel like between her thighs with both of them naked.

He held her as she found her footing and then released her. His body brushed against her back as he moved around her. Watching him head for the server who'd wound up on the floor, her filled tray now covering the very gorgeous man sitting in the booth across from Luminous Smile man, Libby realized he wasn't that much taller than her.

She was decently tall compared to the average woman, but he only had an inch or two on her.

"Ana, are you okay? Melody, stop laughing already."

"Oh my god. I am so sorry." The server, the one who'd given her the warning about cash, knelt down on the floor, her face in her hands.

A woman with harsh features came out of the kitchen as the other servers were working to clean up the mess. The rest of the restaurant just went on with their eating. The server on the floor, Ana, looked up at the woman from the kitchen. "I'm so sorry, Nancy."

Nancy's deep voice rumbled clear as day, even though Libby could tell she was trying to keep it low. "As long as no one's hurt, food can be replaced. We'll talk about it later. Let's just get this cleaned up."

Ana nodded, and Lap Man helped pull her up from the floor. The man covered in food was calmly stacking the plates and bowls that had been dumped on him on the table. Within minutes, most everything was sorted.

Nancy looked around, and pointed at Libby and the other two tables involved. "Your meals are on the house."

"But..."

"No buts. Leave a tip for Bob, and we're good. If you need to break a bill, Lydia can help you."

Not wanting to argue, Libby just nodded.

The other two tables must be regulars as they said nothing, just went about with what they were doing. Well, not Melanie—Melody?—whatever her name, she was still in her chair chuckling.

Libby turned to head to the register, but she caught sight of Luminous Smile and he was staring at Mel-whatever. Kind of like the fish her grandfather had caught the one time he'd taken her out on the boat.

Deciding all this was not her business, she headed to the register and waited. Lydia, the Black server, finally came up. "Sorry about that. Ana's not the most coordinated."

"It's all good. It sounded like something was happening right before she knocked into me."

"Someone tried getting her attention, and got it, but her head went one way while her feet were still going in the original direction. Happens weekly, but not usually when she's got a completely full tray fresh from the kitchen."

Libby glanced over to where the other server, Ana, was working to clean up the mess. The men in the booth were both calmly sitting there and helping to clean up what they could. If this had happened in New York, whoever had been covered in food would probably be calling the cops for assault. Instead, those two gorgeous men were just swiping food and other debris into a container.

She glanced around the dining room. This entire town

was filled with better-looking-than-average people. It must be something in the water. Probably a lot less stress.

Pulling her wallet out of her purse, she grabbed the one bill left. "I'm sorry, but can you break a fifty? That's all I have."

Lydia pulled a marker from a pen cup next to the register. "Normally we don't take more than twenties, but considering what happened, I'll allow it this once. You sticking around town?"

"For a little bit. I came to visit someone, and as soon as I see them, I'm heading back home." Back home, where she'd have to face the consequences. It wasn't fair to Greer to dump the initial reaction on her shoulders, but Greer seemed almost giddy about it.

"Overnight?"

"If I can find a hotel room."

"Tell you what. We close at three, so if you promise to stop back in before then, I'll go ahead and take this. I'll send Ana over to the bank after the morning rush to make sure this is good. If it isn't, you'll have time to get us sorted."

"Deal."

"What's your name?"

"Libby Hartwell."

"Welcome to Sunflower Falls, Libby Hartwell."

They exchanged bills, and Libby left a ten for Bob. She headed back out to the parking lot and was getting ready to pull out when she saw Lap Man and Melody—Melanie?—walking past. They got into a dark blue pickup truck with a white logo on the door that was parked on the street. Libby was about to pull out of the parking lot when the truck pulled out and headed down the road in front of her.

"Asshole." Probably thought because they were local, they didn't have to think about anyone else. She shook her head and focused on the rest of the traffic.

Sunflower Falls wasn't tiny, but it also wasn't a huge town. She assumed the houses that lined the lake were more for vacationers and tourists. Realizing she didn't know where she was going, she pulled over into a parking lot for the public access beach. This far north and this early in the summer, she wondered how cold the water was. But the lot was more than half full, so enough people were willing to brave any coldness.

She'd taken nothing with her when she'd decided to run, so all she had was the photo she'd taken of the envelope in case she needed it for evidence. The handwriting wasn't the best, so she zoomed in on the picture.

After three tries, she finally got the right street entered into the navigation system. She was only a five-minute drive away.

This time, no assholes blocked her path onto the road, and she was pulling up in front of a small, single-family home on a quiet street five minutes later, as promised.

Libby adjusted the rear-view mirror so she could examine herself. Her makeup was smudged and her lipstick long chewed off. Not the best of first impressions, but she was who she was. A runaway bride in search of her mother's past.

Sometimes, she wondered if her mother had wished she'd run away.

Libby blew out a breath and got out of the car. The front door looked like it could use a fresh coat of paint, but otherwise, everything seemed in good condition to her unpracticed eye.

After a moment of searching, she finally found the doorbell and rang it. The bell was a lovely set of three notes. But after a bit, she realized no one was coming to the door. She rang again.

The three notes filled the air. But that was it. No dog

barking. No yells from the back of the house that they were coming.

Pure silence.

She opened the screen door and knocked. It likely wasn't going to make a difference, but she had to try. She'd come all this way. Blown off her own damn wedding. She wanted answers.

"Can I help you?"

She turned around to find Lap Man and Melanie—Melody?—standing on the front lawn, looking at her.

Libby stepped away from the screen door, letting it slam closed. "Do you live here?"

"No. Our uncle does. What do you want?"

"To talk with him. When is he coming back?"

"In July. Come back then."

two

ERIC HEARD A COUGH BEHIND HIM AND KNEW THAT MELODY WAS covering a snicker. She could barely stop laughing after what happened at the diner this morning, even though her best friend had been at the center of the ruckus.

He ignored his baby sister for a moment and focused on the gorgeous woman in front of him.

Gorgeous woman who was wearing a blazing engagement ring. He'd noticed her when she came into the diner, and, out of habit thanks to living in a town with a lot of tourists rolling through, checked for a ring. As soon as he spotted it, he put her out of his mind.

If there was one thing Uncle Stef had drilled into him since time immemorial, it was that hooking up with women who wore engagement or wedding rings wasn't worth the heartache.

Then she found her way into his lap through no fault of her own.

His body perked up in ways that it shouldn't be perking up for a woman who was not available.

She was gone by the time he left Ana in Nancy's more-than-capable hands, and he hadn't expected to see her again.

But here she was. Knocking on Uncle Stef's front door.

"What do you mean, he's gone until July?"

Even her voice was pretty. A sweet tone that has just enough huskiness to catch a man's attention.

"Exactly what I said. Come back then if you want to see him."

"I can't come back."

This time, he heard a note of panic in her words. What was going on with her? "Well, he's not answering anyone until he comes back. This is his vacation. No one's allowed to know where he is, and we don't bother him."

"But he wrote to me. I need answers."

Uncle Stef? Wrote to her? The man who communicated as little as possible? Actually took up pen and paper and wrote to someone who Eric didn't know existed?

He hooked his thumbs in the belt loops of his work pants. "About what?"

"My mother."

Melody's cough was decidedly a cough this time. She cleared her throat. "Our Uncle Stef isn't known for writing. Why would he write to you about your mother? And why isn't she here asking for herself?"

Eric caught the slight wince on the woman's face before she squared her shoulders. And why was she wearing clothes that looked better suited to a nightclub? Where had she come from? "Melody."

"Listen, Uncle Stef's not the most talkative guy. Why would he actually write something down? He barely signs his own damn contracts."

"That would explain the handwriting."

Melody pointed at the other woman. "That. The man's handwriting's atrocious. And I say this with absolute love, but if he could get away with just stamping a heart in our birthday cards, he would."

Eric realized this conversation was getting away from him. "Look, leave a message with us, and we'll get it to him when he comes back to town. You can go back to wherever you came from."

Melody smacked the back of his head. "You did not just say that."

"What?"

"Use your brain and think it over." She grinned at the woman. "Hi, my name's Melody Keller, and this socially incompetent next to me is my brother Eric."

"Uh, nice to meet you?"

If he'd been faced with Melody's brand of hospitality, he would have been questioning the joy of meeting her, too. But there was also photographic evidence of him questioning her arrival on his doorstep when he was barely a year old.

"Listen, we need to get going. Why don't you go home and come back in July."

"I can't."

Save him from people who lived to make his life harder. "I don't care that you can't. Just leave. He's not here. We need to take care of some things and get to work."

The lady without a name got that look on her face that told him she was going to be trouble. At least he and Melody had every legal right to be here. He didn't even know that Uncle Stef had even written to her. But she did know about his pretty much illegible writing.

"Fine. I need a place to stay. What's available around here?"

Before he could say anything, Melody whipped out her phone. "Are you going to stay through to July?"

The lady—he did *not* want to find out her name—twisted that engagement ring around her finger. "Yes."

He swallowed a growl. "Melody."

She waved her hand at him. "Go take care of that thing. I'll help...what is your name?"

"Libby Hartwell."

"Nice to meet you, Libby. Ignore my caveman brother."

He shook his head and went around the back of the house. One of the neighbors called him last night saying that something had gotten knocked down by the wind as they'd heard a loud clattering come from Uncle Stef's.

It took him only a few minutes to find the screen that had been wrenched from its tracks. He'd told Stef over and over that he needed to upgrade his windows. Despite being well known as part of the cast of one of the longest home renovation shows, his uncle took frugality almost to miserly.

He pulled out his keys and went down into the cellar to grab the ladder Uncle Stef kept in there. Ten minutes later, he had the screen back in its tracks. He pushed the aluminum back into place. It wouldn't keep the screen in place in the next heavy wind, but as soon as Uncle Stef was back from wherever he went for his summer break, Eric was taking him shopping for new windows.

Melody came around the corner of the house as he was opening the door to put the ladder back. "What was it? The screen that won't stay in place?"

"You got it in one. Did you get rid of her?"

Melody's brows rose. "You're certainly in a surly attitude this morning? What happened? Maxwell shit in your shoes again?"

Eric shook his head and focused on putting away the ladder.

"Awwww. You know that cat loves you."

"That cat is a hellspawn. I don't know why Mom keeps him around."

"Cats are great."

"Dogs are great. Cats are plotting our demise."

Melody laughed. "Come on. What gives?"

He focused on locking the door. Before they left, he should make sure that everything was locked up tight. Especially after the call he'd gotten this morning.

Melody tackle-hugged him from behind. "Come on, big brother. You're not usually such an asshole to the tourists."

"Did you get her sorted out?"

She pinched his arm. "I'll get it out of you one way or another."

"Mel. Not now."

"Fine. Yes, I got her all sorted. She's going to stay at the Sunflower Motel."

"Jesus, no."

"Yep. You know it's the best place there is."

"I don't want Mom getting involved."

"Too late. Mom's expecting her. She'll get Libby sorted out and all the juicy gossip about why she can't go home."

Eric closed his eyes. Why? Why all this? He rubbed his brow. There was nothing he could do about it at the moment, which meant he needed to get to work. "Get in the truck."

Melody saluted him, "Aye, aye, Captain Bligh."

He ignored her like he did every time she pulled that. As he walked around the bed of the truck, he realized he'd need to make sure that all the tools they kept stored in it were locked up every night. He didn't need to wake up one morning to discover their father had decided to make a quick buck.

Barely ten minutes later, he pulled into one of the two

parking spaces behind the storefront office he and Melody used as their home base.

Melody was out of the truck first and had the back door open. "You know we need to hire someone, right?"

"You say that every time we're in the office."

"Because every time we walk in the office, I'm once again confronted by the fact that we need an office manager."

"So hire one."

"You banned me from hiring any office help after last time."

"He was stealing the petty cash, Melody."

"But he was saving up for classes at the community college." She tossed her work bag down on her desk. It was mostly clear except for the flat screen monitor.

He looked at his own desk. Catalogs, some client files, and mail littered the entire surface. Melody wasn't wrong about their needing help, but she also wasn't right, either.

"Just focus on getting the monthlies up-to-date. We need to get over to the Sullivan site by noon."

Melody sighed, but didn't say anything.

He woke up his own computer and cursed. An email had come in from the management company he was in talks with. They had to reschedule the meeting again.

Grabbing a flyer he knew was garbage, he balled it up as tight as he could and lofted it into the garbage can.

Melody looked up. "What happened?"

"B&H had to reschedule. Again."

"So?"

"If they want our business, they need to stop dicking me around like this."

Melody let her head fall back. "Can *you* not be such a dick?" She looked up and glared at him. "What has gotten into you? You're always doing a fair imitation of Oscar, but you're like his older, ten-times-worse cousin today."

She deserved to know. And worse, needed to be warned. "Dad's back."

"Okay. I'll carry a nail gun around with me and maim him if he gets too close."

He stared at her. She was as calm as if he'd told her the special at the diner was going to be chicken and waffles. "That's it?"

"Of course that's it. The asshole is always crawling back around when he needs money. Give Mom a head's up." Melody shook her head and turned back to her screen.

Eric knew that wasn't it. Their dad had run out of town when Eric had been six and Melody five. She'd just had her birthday party, and he'd taken every single dollar she'd received. Their grandparents had disowned him, and Uncle Stef had stepped in, but he was still their dad.

"And don't you dare refuse to reschedule with B&H. We need them."

Eric pulled up the plans for the Sullivan remodel. He knew Melody was right, but he wasn't in the most pleasant frame of mind to deal with the management company.

After reviewing the plans, he still wanted to flame his contact, so he threaded his fingers together behind his head and stared out onto the street. Saturday mornings in Sunflower Falls were pretty busy, and there were a fair amount of people walking past the plate-glass window. One stopped and put her hands on either side of her face, peering in.

He groaned.

Melody looked up, switched her attention to the front, and waved.

When she got up, he jacked forward in his seat. "Do not let her in, Melody."

She flipped him the bird and then flipped the lock open. "Hey, Libby. What are you doing here?"

"I was passing by on my way to Secrets and Whimsies and wondered why this place looked closed when everything else was open."

Melody jerked her thumb in his direction. "I'm babysitting the king of the grouches. Better we limit interaction with him. Besides, this is more of an office than a storefront."

Hartwell looked around. He gave her credit for not sneering or anything. "I can see."

"Hey, we need an office manager. Need a temporary job while you're waiting for Uncle Stef?"

"Melody."

"Shut it. You gave me hiring powers. I'm trying to hire here."

Hartwell laughed, and it did things to his gut that he did not want to think about.

"I've already got a job. In fact, I need to check in with my partner."

"Partner? What do you do?"

Hartwell crossed her arms around her middle. "We're just getting off the ground with some clients. I went to law school."

Melody whistled. "An honest-to-God attorney. We've got a few around here. I guess you don't want to be filing papers for us with a degree like that."

Hartwell's features hardened. "There's nothing wrong with filing papers. We're small, so we had to do all the clerical work for ourselves before we could afford to bring on our own office manager."

Melody grinned. "I like you. And you're right, nothing wrong with doing the work. It's just that we're taking on more projects than we can handle *and* do all the office work. Big brother here is not the neatest person as you can see."

He cleared his throat. "I do fine."

"As long as you're the only person looking for paperwork."

Hartwell relaxed a bit as they bickered. He wondered if she had siblings. In his experience, the people he knew without siblings didn't know what to do when he and Melody got into it. "She's not looking for a job, and she was heading somewhere else. Let her go, already."

Hartwell narrowed her eyes. "Trying to get rid of me?"

He crossed his own arms against his chest. Saw her gaze linger a little on his biceps. Considering she was still wearing that damn ring, his already low opinion of her knocked down a little more. "So what if I am?"

"Jesus, Eric. Knock it off. Libby, if you're going to be in town for a month and decide you even want to do some part-time work, let us know."

Eric's computer pinged. He looked at the incoming email and scowled.

"What now?"

He glanced at Melody before opening the email. "B&H. They need to change the reschedule dates."

"So? Did you even respond to the first request?"

"B&H?" Hartwell's voice had gone a little high there with the question.

Eric looked over at Melody, who had her "I have questions" face on. He looked back at Hartwell. "They're an entertainment management consulting firm we're thinking of working with."

"I thought you were in construction or something?"

The office didn't have the best lighting, but Eric swore her face had a green tinge to it. "We are. But we're also in negotiations to have our own show."

Melody leaned back on her desk. "Both of us were on Uncle Stef's show before we started our own company."

"Show?"

Yeah, she definitely was looking a little sick. What was her problem? Did she not like to associate with people who might have a camera crew after them? Was she hiding from someone? "To The Bones. It's been on for thirty years."

"I've heard of it." She cleared her throat, and the green dialed down a little.

"So why freak out about B&H?" Melody tapped her fingers against the pressed wood of her desktop.

Hartwell waved. "Hi. I'm H."

Melody had a coughing fit.

Eric glared at her. "Prove it."

"Your contact is Greer Branford. She handles all the client-side work and is probably dealing with the cancellation of my wedding on top of trying to reschedule the meeting with you."

Her wedding was canceled. He forced away the lift those few words gave him. It was none of his business if her wedding was canceled or just postponed.

Eric scowled. "Why haven't we spoken with you?"

She waved her left hand. "Hello, I had a wedding I was preparing for? Besides, I deal with the contracts and other stuff once the clients have been on-boarded. Greer's better at enticing clients to come on board."

"You're why she's trying to reschedule."

"What?"

"I told her I needed to meet with all the principles. She emailed this morning, letting me know she needed to reschedule from the Monday meeting we had set, and just emailed again saying that she had to push potential dates even further out."

"That is not my fault."

"That is completely your fault."

She pursed her lips, and she looked like she was biting back words. "Why are you even bothering with us if you don't like the way we run our business?"

"Yeah, big brother, why are you even bothering with them?"

He glared at Melody. "Stop shit stirring."

She grinned back at him. "But it's so much fun."

He wanted to tell Hartwell to just leave and he wouldn't be bothering with them, but he couldn't. They needed B&H's services. Despite apparently being small as hell, they also had one of the best reputations for up-and-coming talent management, both with the television industry and social media influencers. He didn't want to bother with that side of things, so that was another duty he'd tossed in Melody's lap.

It was a necessary evil, as far as he was concerned.

"What big brother here doesn't want to admit to is that his attitude has caused him to be declared *difficult*." Melody made air quotes as she said the last word. "But apparently you guys have a reputation for working well with difficult clients."

"It's all about the client's goals. As long as we're in alignment, and the potential client isn't a complete and total asshole," she definitely was pointedly looking at him, "we can work with anyone that we think we can help."

Eric began to reply, but before he could do so, she held up a finger. "In fact, I do have a say over who we take on as clients. I haven't talked with Greer yet about your firm. I'm sure she was waiting for this wedding to be over, but I can let her know that I've met with you."

He heard calculation in her tone. "And what?"

"And I can tell her one of two things."

He crossed his arms against his chest again. And again

didn't miss the way her gaze followed the move. "Those two things would be what?"

"That you're either a dream to work with or that I give the thumbs down."

He narrowed his eyes. This definitely was a negotiation. She may be a lawyer, but he'd been haggling over construction supplies for his uncle for the last fifteen years. "What would it take for you to say the former?"

She grinned at him and it hit like Tucker Yancy did when he'd been feet away from the winning touchdown at the state finals. "Stop trying to run me out of town and let me know immediately when you hear from your uncle."

"Deal."

"Melody." He winced, as he knew the shout had been too much.

"Shush. You had your say." She walked over to Hartwell and held out a hand. "Shake on it."

Hartwell did. But Melody held on when she went to pull away.

Melody leaned in. "What do you even want to talk to Uncle Stef about?"

Hartwell briefly glanced away from Melody to meet his own gaze. He lifted a brow, and she didn't look away from him. "I need to know my mother's secrets."

three

LIBBY WALKED PAST THE FEW STOREFRONTS THERE WERE BETWEEN the Kellers' office and Secrets and Whimsies. As promised, the door was open.

When she walked in, the variety of offerings overwhelmed her. Mrs. Smith was truly leaning into the whimsy portion of the name.

"Be right with you."

"Take your time." Libby wandered over to a little alcove which held a variety of candles and other scents. Each candle contained some kind of crystal that you could retrieve once you had burned it down, but you didn't know what the crystal was until you retrieved it.

"Ah, Ms. Hartwell."

She turned around and found Mrs. Smith standing behind her with her hands clasped together. "This is an interesting shop."

"I'm glad you think so. It keeps me busy in my retirement."

"Oh? What did you do?"

"I mainly talked to people." She grinned. "Now, I'm

guessing you're not in here for aromatherapy or crystal divination."

Libby laughed. "No. I'm just getting a sense of the town. I'm going to be here longer than I originally planned."

Mrs. Smith began walking away and waved for Libby to follow. "You must share. Would you like some tea? I have an excellent supply from a friend."

Libby wasn't much of a tea person, especially in summer, but as Mrs. Smith had been so welcoming to her —unlike a certain, surly whatever he was—it would have been impolite to refuse.

"Thank you."

Mrs. Smith closed the entry door and flipped the sign to closed. "We get little traffic in the mornings, anyway."

Libby wondered why that was since it was a Saturday and she'd seen a lot of people wandering around while she explored. "Isn't that unusual?"

"Not in Sunflower Falls. My shop is fairly new, so people are still figuring me out along with the shop. And the beginning of tourist season isn't until the Start of Summer Street Fair in a couple weeks. We wait until the children are fully out of school."

"That sounds like fun."

Mrs. Smith laughed. "You're not that convincing. Take it from a pro." She opened a door in back, which led to a comfortable, if small, office area. "Now, do you have a flavor preference?"

Libby shook her head. "Honestly, I'm not a tea person, so whatever you serve will be fine, I'm sure."

"I do appreciate honesty. It was scarce in my previous line of work."

Before Libby could question that, Mrs. Smith opened a small cabinet by the desk and pulled out a container of tea bags. She then flipped on what looked to be a very complicated kettle.

"Have a seat, Libby. I don't believe I mentioned that I know your father?"

Libby blinked. This woman knew her father? Was her running away going to be for nothing because of who she happened to sit next to at breakfast?

Her panic must have shown on her face because Mrs. Smith was shaking her head. "I know him, but not well enough to randomly get in contact with him. Besides. You seem like a very interesting person, and I'd like to get to know you better."

Never had one of her father's acquaintances called her "interesting". More often than not, they actually or figuratively patted her on the head and ignored her. Libby's law school years would have been even more tortuous if it hadn't been for Greer. Though Greer was in the combined MBA/JD program, so they hadn't had as many courses together as Libby would have liked.

Libby blew out a breath. "How do you know my father?"

Mrs. Smith smiled. "Oh, here and there. I used to run in some interesting circles, though I'm sure your father rarely took notice of me on the fringes."

If Mrs. Smith had stayed on the fringes, then there was every reason to believe that her father had barely noticed her unless someone specifically drew his attention to her. Her father enjoyed the spotlight and others who also cultivated it.

"Sugar, honey, cream?"

Libby shook her head. "Nothing. Thank you."

Mrs. Smith began talking about the upcoming street fair, and Libby managed to relax in the small visitor's chair. "You'll want to check it out. That nice Eric Keller—the man whose lap you ended up in this morning—usually has a booth where they do demonstrations of home renovation projects."

Libby sat up. "Eric Keller? Why should I pay attention to him?" Had Mrs. Smith somehow divined why she was in town and that she had been at the Kellers' before coming here?

Mrs. Smith took a sip of her tea. Libby narrowed her eyes. Was the woman laughing at her?

The older woman cleared her throat. "He's a bit of a celebrity thanks to his uncle and *his* friends having Eric, Melody, and some others in the next generation on their show the last few years."

"I've never been much into home renovation." Her father had nipped any interest in home projects in the bud when she'd been a child. He declared he was raising the next generation of Hartwell lawyers, even if she were a girl. Father of the year right there.

Once she'd gotten somewhat out from under his thumb, she'd been too busy setting up her firm with Greer to watch many shows beyond those done by potential clients. And with the wedding, she hadn't exactly been pulling her weight with even that for the last few months.

Libby took a sip of her own tea.

"I will say, I always do enjoy spotting one of the workers with their shirt off. It doesn't happen often on the shows, so I savor it when I can."

Libby did her absolute best to not spray the other woman with hot tea. She choked down the mouthful and cleared her throat. "I haven't watched."

Mrs. Smith toasted her with her teacup. "It's even better live and in person. Since you'll be in town for a while, you really should spend a day down near the lakefront. I believe the Kellers are currently renovating the Sullivan property."

Humming, Libby went back to her tea even as she made a note to herself to keep as much information about herself close to the chest around this woman. "I'm not interested in anyone right now." She wiggled her left ring finger for emphasis. "I'm currently getting out of a relationship."

Mrs. Smith grinned. "I do remember. My philosophy has always been that a good rebound is worth breaking a few bed slats."

This time, Libby sent up a prayer of thanksgiving to a deity she didn't particularly believe in that she hadn't been sipping her tea. No way would she have been able to avoid baptizing her host. "I should probably go."

Mrs. Smith smiled. "I look forward to seeing you around town. There's a lot for people to do in our little town. It's also a wonderful place to quiet yourself away and reset your life, if that's your intention."

The way the woman seemed to divine her thoughts weirded Libby out a bit, but she also had the clear sense that Mrs. Smith was encouraging her to figure out what it meant to fully step out of the shadow of Gregory Hartwell, the Third.

As she left Secrets and Whimsies, a cool breeze cut through the air. She drew in a deep breath and could smell the lake along with some of the flowers, which were beginning to bloom in the sidewalk container gardens lining the street.

It really was time for her to move on with her life. But she also needed the space to build her defenses against her father. Which meant she needed to get in contact with Greer.

Deciding it was time for a drive, she headed back to the motel and pulled out her car keys. According to her phone, there was a big box store about an hour away. She could get the beginning necessities for spending a month in Sunflower Falls there.

Once she hit the town limits, she called Greer.

Her best friend picked up just as Libby expected the call to switch over to voicemail. "Hey, Dustin. I'm busy right now. Can I call you back in five?"

Realizing Greer was with someone who she didn't want to know that it was Libby on the other end of the line, she lowered her voice as much as possible and grumbled a "Sure."

Greer hung up immediately.

Libby took the opportunity to check out the roads she was driving on and waited until Greer called back fifteen minutes later. "I am so sorry. Your father stormed in here, demanding to know where you were."

"I'm sorry, Greer."

"Hey, I volunteered for this. Believe me, it gave me great pleasure to tell him you were off dealing with your feelings and didn't want to talk with anyone."

There was something in Greer's gleeful tone that had Libby wondering if something else happened besides everyone suddenly discovering the bride had disappeared. "Still, he can be a runaway train when he's not getting his way."

"And he'll continue to not get his way. I've got your phone powered down and stuck in my winter sweaters bin."

It had been Greer who'd come up with the cloak-and-dagger tactics to get Libby sort of off the grid. The only thing they couldn't help was that Libby was in Greer's car, so if her father decided to track her using that, she wasn't sure what to do. She hoped he would try to save face by writing her off.

"I'm staying, Greer."

"What? Where? Permanently?"

For the first time in what felt like eons, Libby laughed. "No. I'm staying in Sunflower Falls for about a month. Maybe a little bit longer. The man I came to see is off on some hermit vacation."

"Hunh. Well, find some guy to fuck in the meantime. You deserve it."

"Greer! I'm not looking for some guy to fuck. I just ran away from my own damn wedding."

"Mm-hmmmm."

There was that tone again. "Greer? What aren't you telling me?"

Greer let out a long breath. "Nothing you can deal with at this point, so don't worry about it. You know Four wasn't worth it."

"He wasn't bad."

"Libby. You're trying to justify. The man agreed to marry you to advance his career. Your father bribed him. Whether or not he's a bad guy in the overall sense, he made some extremely shitty decisions. I don't know why you even said yes to him."

Libby hunched her shoulders. "I told you. I was feeling lonely. I thought we had something in common with parental expectations. He didn't make me feel as lonely."

Greer sighed. "I know. I know, Libby. But you deserve the world. You're one of the sweetest people I know, and for being an absolute wonder at negotiating contracts and protecting our clients, you put too much faith in others."

"Not my father."

"Of course not your father. No one really trusts your dad. And with good reason. Now, seriously, go find some farmer or whatever they have up there and fuck him silly. Find yourself a sex life."

"Don't you mean love life?"

"No. This is rebound time." What was it with people advising her to sleep with someone as a rebound activity?

"Except I didn't really love Herman." And that was the worst thing of all. She'd liked him, kind of, but the fact she'd been so starved for affection that she'd agreed to marry him when she didn't love him made her one of the worst kinds of users. They both deserved better.

"Which makes me ecstatic that you came to your senses before the wedding and ran off. How many times have I told you that deposits are cheaper than divorce?"

That had been Greer's motto since law school. They met on the first day as they sat in class, and one of the other students proposed in an elaborate display to another student. Greer had turned to Libby and said. "She'd better wise up. Deposits are cheaper than divorce, and he just made this all about him."

Greer had stood up in several weddings since then, but every time, she made a point to avoid being in a serious relationship or catching the bouquet. Marriage was not for her.

"All the time, Greer. All the time. I should talk to Herman."

"No!" Greer cleared her throat. "I've got it handled. Believe me. As your legal representative, it's better if I handle this."

"You're my legal representative?"

"We're partners. We represent each other."

Libby knew that wasn't how things worked, but if she could avoid having to deal with Herman for a bit longer, she'd fake it. "Thanks, Greer."

"You're my sister from another mother. Until pigs fly and your dad turns the firm to one-hundred percent pro bono work. Now, your dad is obviously trying to track you, so give me an address or something, and I'll send you a bunch of those credit gift cards. Consider this an enforced vacation and don't worry about anything. I've got it handled."

It was Libby's turn to clear her throat. "Um, speaking of vacation…"

"What?"

"I met a prospective client."

"Seriously?" Greer laughed. "I thought we agreed I'd do all the prospecting?"

"You already have."

"What?"

Libby slowed for a stoplight. "I've met your latest set of prospects. The Kellers."

Greer hummed. "You know…we haven't signed them yet. You could hook up with Eric."

"Greer. No. We're in negotiations with him."

"I'm in negotiations with him."

"On behalf of the business. Of which I am a partner. No. I already outed myself to him. And…" She trailed off. And she'd already taken advantage of the power she held over him. Damn it.

"And what?"

"And I basically bribed him with the possibility of us representing him if he stopped trying to run me out of town."

Greer laughed. "Good for you. He's a hardass, so I'm sure it barely phased him. I'll get on the phone with him later to discuss things."

"If you think we can be of benefit to them, I have no issues with representing them. I want to make that explicitly clear."

"You have. But, seriously, if not Eric, find someone else in town to bang. Get Four out of your system and have fun with this new phase of your life. You're free, Libby. Totally free."

"Thanks, Greer. I need to go buy some clothes. I'll check in tomorrow."

"Have some fun, Libby. Whatever you need to do."

They hung up. As she went into the store, all Libby could think of was Greer's comments about being free. She wasn't truly free. She never had been. Her family's past had always weighed her down in one way or another. And she was most definitely a Hartwell. Her father had given her the results of the various paternity tests he'd had commissioned over her childhood on her eighteenth birthday, along with the partial access to her portion of the family trust she was entitled to.

Seriously, a class act all the way.

She kept her purchases to the absolute minimum she needed to get through until Greer sent the new gift cards. With that thought in mind, she got some basic food items as well. She couldn't blow all her money on eating out, even if it was cheap.

Once she was back on the road to Sunflower Falls, she rolled down the windows and turned on some of her favorite music. She was rocking out to the latest release from her favorite singer when she spotted a dog sitting on the side of the road.

Slowing down, she pulled over onto the gravel shoulder. It wasn't big as it turned to tall-ish grass and then woods. As far as she could tell, there wasn't any housing nearby. And the dog was still just sitting there, staring at her.

She checked the rearview mirror, but no one else was on the road. The dog continued to stare at her.

Easing the door open, she put one foot out. Still no

movement from the dog. She expected it to run off, but it steadily watched her.

Its coat was matted with some dirt and other debris. The poor thing had probably been out here for a while.

She couldn't quite tell what kind of dog other than it had the look of a lab or golden in the face. Even when she closed the door, it continued to sit and stare at her.

"Are you okay? Do you need help?"

It cocked its head. When she got to the front of the car and stopped, it finally got up and moved closer to her. When it stopped a couple feet away from her, Libby slowly crouched down and then held out her hand, palm down.

The dog sniffed her hand and then placed its head under it. "You poor thing. Do you want a ride?"

To where, though? Was there a vet around here some-where? She petted the dog for a few more minutes, and its tail was wagging. "Okay. Let's get in the car."

The dog chuffed and then bounded off into the woods. "What the hell?" She stood there for a minute, unsure what to do. Then she saw the dog come back out of the brush carrying something in its mouth. Once it got closer, she heard tiny yips and realized it was a puppy. The dog came up to her and sat down.

"Oh, sweet baby." She crouched down and once again held out her hand, palm down. The dog nudged her hand with its muzzle and the puppy, so she reached out with her other hand and cupped them together. The dog dropped the puppy in her hands and then headed back into the woods.

Libby looked down at the puppy. It yawned and then snuggled into her hands. "This has got to be a dream." She heard rustling again and saw the dog return with yet another puppy in its mouth.

As soon as the dog sat down, she held out her hand. The second puppy was deposited into her care. "Any more?"

The dog barked.

"Okay, I'm going to put them in the backseat. You go get the rest."

The dog seemed to understand her as it headed back to wherever it had stashed the puppies.

She opened the back passenger door while cradling both puppies in her other arm. As soon as she got them settled onto the seat, she went to the trunk to see if she could find anything to place them in. She lucked out with a box that was filled with car gear. She dumped the contents into the trunk and went back around to the open door. The dog was back with a third puppy.

"I'll get them settled. How many more do you have?"

Apparently, despite understanding her, the dog couldn't count. It went back into the woods as soon as she took number three from it.

She situated the box on the seat and buckled it in. The puppies probably needed something warmer than empty cardboard. She looked at them and then grabbed her bag of goodies from the big box store. "You're lucky you're cute."

After lining the bottom of the box with the athletic pullover she'd bought, she carefully transferred all three puppies into the box. Two were limp, but breathing, so she assumed they felt safe enough to nap.

She had just placed the third in the box when the dog turned up again with number four. "Any more?"

It yipped as soon as she took possession of the new one and headed back into the woods.

"I hope whatever you bring back is the last one."

The dog came back within minutes with a much-smaller-than-the-others puppy. This one seemed to have trouble breathing. She carefully took hold of the puppy and placed it into the box. Instead of heading back into the woods again, the dog slipped between her legs and climbed into the car. It situated itself on the free part of the seat, its head propped up on the edge of the box.

"You ready?"

It woofed, and Libby took it for agreement. She drove back to Sunflower Falls as slow as was reasonable, not wanting to get in an accident with her precious cargo.

She glanced back as they entered the town limits. "I'm going to need help, aren't I?"

The dog woofed again.

four

"MOM, I WANT YOU TO TAKE THIS SERIOUSLY." ERIC WATCHED AS his mother filed paperwork.

"Eric, I know exactly the kind of person your father is. You don't have to worry about me if he shows up. Believe me, he will curse the day he ever met me if he shows up."

He rubbed his forehead, though that did nothing for the headache that was forming there. "Mom, just him showing up can cause trouble."

His mom looked up from the file she was flipping through. She reached out and clasped his hand. "Honey, I know you're worried about him. But worrying this much about what he might do just sucks away your energy and gives him power." She squeezed his hand. "I want you to focus on your work, and what you're building with Melody."

"Him coming back will remind everyone that I'm his son. I don't want them to think I may take after him." The way *he* thought he might take after his dad if he didn't keep himself on a tight leash.

His mom stood up, cupped his face, and pulled it down so she could smack a kiss against his forehead. "You always were my serious little man. There is no way you could ever take after your father in temperament."

"I look like him."

"Eric, just because you look like him doesn't mean that you take after him in any way beyond that. Do I need to start nagging you again about seeing a therapist?"

He blew out a breath. "No." Probably. He usually did fine when his dad stayed away. But the odd times he blew back into town? Yeah. Not great.

There was a rustling at the motel's front door, and they both turned around. It was Hartwell, and she was trying to open the door while carrying a box.

He went over and pushed the door open.

She blew up a breath of air that moved the lock of hair that had fallen out of the ponytail she had her hair pulled back into, but it just flopped back to where it had fallen. "Thanks. This is not easy."

He was about to let the door close behind her when the mangiest mutt he'd ever seen trotted in after her. "What…"

Then he looked down into the box. Five more mutts of the puppy variety were sound asleep in it.

"What the hell?"

"Eric. Language."

Since he was facing away from his mom, he rolled his eyes.

"Hi, Mrs. Keller. I didn't want to leave these guys in the car, but I need to know where a vet's office is around here."

Eric watched as his mom flew around the reception desk and peered into the box. "Oh, aren't they the cutest?"

She looked down at the dog, who had sat down next to Hartwell as soon as she'd stopped moving. "And you're so well behaved. Is this the mother?"

Hartwell shrugged, but managed not to jostle the box too much. "Probably? I didn't really think to check. It was

39

sitting on the side of the road, and I pulled over to see if I could help it. Then it brought all these little guys out of the woods to me."

"Oh, my. What a good parent you are." His mom crouched down and held out a hand for the dog to sniff.

The dog deigned to check her out, and then let her pet. But he didn't miss that the dog didn't move too far from Hartwell's side. Whether it was because she was holding the puppies or what, he didn't know.

Realizing that this could go on all day if he didn't do something, he cleared his throat.

She threw him an annoyed glance. "What do you want?"

"I can get you in at the vet. Come on."

"Just like that?"

"Yeah."

She looked back at his mom. "Is he serious?"

"Yep. He and Sam went to high school and college together. If he calls, Sam will get him on the schedule." She continued petting the dog. "I promise, Sam will take excellent care of you and your babies."

The dog looked over at him and woofed. It was kind of eerie.

"Okay. Let's go."

"Mom, do you have any towels I can borrow?"

"Sure. I'll meet you outside. Get the puppies buckled in."

He held the door for Hartwell, and while they waited for his mom to come out, he called up the vet practice. As promised, they squeezed him in, though they'd likely have to wait for a bit. Saturdays were the busiest day for the practice. Sam was already talking about needing to bring in a partner now that old Doc Jinx had retired.

His mom came out the side door of the office carrying

an armload of towels. He took them from her and lined the back seat of his truck with them before taking the box of puppies from Hartwell and buckling them in. The dog leaped in when he stepped to the side and settled on the seat next to the box. Hartwell climbed up into the passenger seat before he could offer a hand.

Walking around the front of the truck, he shook his head. Good deeds never went unpunished. His mom waved at them. "Have fun. Tell Sam I said hello."

"Will do." He climbed into the truck before she could say anything else.

They accomplished the fifteen-minute ride in silence. Thanks to the practice caring for livestock in addition to Sunflower Falls' pet population, they had five acres on the other end of town from the lake.

The gravel parking lot was nearly filled, so he made his own space on the edge, half on the gravel, half on grass. The puppies had been buckled in behind Hartwell, and she had them out before he could get around the truck. Hartwell closed the door with her hip after the dog followed the puppies out.

He looked down at the dog. "She needs to be on a leash before we go in."

Hartwell bit her lip. "I don't know if she's leash trained. Hell, I don't know if she's had any kind of training."

He met the dog's eyes. "Wait." The dog froze. "Hartwell, come over to me."

The dog vibrated as Hartwell walked the couple of feet over to him. "Come." The dog hurried over and stood next to Hartwell. "She's had some training. She wouldn't know those commands otherwise."

"Then we can go in without a leash, right?"

"No. Even the best trained dogs should be on a leash

when outside their own fenced in territory. I'll go in and get a loaner. Wait here for me."

Without waiting for her to respond, he headed into the vet's office. Once in the door, his first check was the small table set off to the right. The candle was off, and he blew out a breath.

The receptionist grinned at him. "Hey, Eric. Where's the emergency?"

"Outside. I need a loaner leash."

"Don't tell me you left a dog in the truck?"

He held up his hands at the murder look Gina shot him. "Hell, no. The dog's outside with a...friend." Hartwell wasn't a friend, but he wasn't sure how to describe her that wouldn't have Gina murdering him with even more eye daggers.

Gina got up and rummaged around in the cabinets behind her. "Harness or collar?"

"Neither."

Gina looked over her shoulder. "What kind of dog do we have?"

"Lab mix, maybe? About fifty pounds. Definitely has some training."

She pulled out a harness and leash. "Try this. If it doesn't work, come back and I'll get you a collar."

He took it from her. "Thanks."

Back outside, the dog was still standing next to Hartwell, exactly where he'd left them. He crouched down and held out the harness for the dog to sniff. She didn't cower away, but he could tell she wasn't a fan, as he felt her vibrating while he put it on. "Come on. Time for everyone to get checked out."

Other than checking the candle, he hadn't paid attention to who else was in the waiting room. When they walked back in, he recognized a few people who'd been in the diner this morning. Including Ralph Winters and his pet pig. Bacon oinked when he spotted the dog and tried to race over.

"Bacon. Sit."

Bacon plopped his butt on the floor, but he continued to oink. Probably trying to entice the dog to come over and play. Of course, Bacon's crooning got the rest of the pets going. At least the ones that could vocalize.

It was into this chaos that Sam came out from the back escorting Brenda Jo Mullaney and her young daughter Holly. Along with Holly's prize-winning cashmere lop rabbit.

The dog quivered next to him. "Wait."

It held still as Brenda Jo finished talking with Sam about caring for a cut the rabbit had gotten and then led Holly out the door.

Sam spotted him. "Hey, man. What's going on?"

"I've got a guest who discovered a stray and a litter of puppies on the side of the road."

Sam frowned and immediately came over to where they stood. He sent Hartwell a smile. "Doctor Sam Rivers at your service."

"Cut it out, Sam. Just look at the puppies."

Sam winked at Hartwell, then turned his attention to the puppies. He picked up each one, doing a quick exam before putting it back in the box. Except for one. For that one, he pulled out a flashlight from his pocket. His hum wasn't particularly reassuring. "Come on back. I want a closer look at this one."

He looked down at the dog. "And we need to get you a wash down." He glanced over at Gina. "When Orna's done with Yazoo, can you have her meet me in exam room three?"

"Sure. Ralph, Bacon will have to wait a little longer."

"If Doc thinks a puppy needs help, that's fine."

They headed back into an exam area and Sam placed the puppy on the exam table. The dog moved to go stand next to him. Before he could hold her back, she jumped up so that her front paws were on the table and she could see the puppy. Sam looked down at her.

"It's okay. She's got some issues, but I'll take care of them."

The dog leaned in and licked the puppy's muzzle. The puppy mewled and tried to crawl over to the dog. Sam petted the puppy's back as he continued to give reassurances to both the dog and Hartwell by extension. The dog wagged its tail and eventually went back down on all fours.

Orna, his vet tech, came into the room a few minutes later. "Orna, can you take the dog and give her a bath, as well as a preliminary examination?"

"Absolutely." She held out a hand for the leash, and Eric handed it over. The dog resisted briefly before Orna crouched down and began petting its neck. "I promise to have you back as soon as possible. Doc will take good care of your little one."

Sam glanced over. "And make sure you scan her for a chip. She definitely has been around humans."

"Will do."

They left with the dog looking back as they exited. The way the dog seemed to understand everything they said really had him wondering who would let such an intelligent dog go loose out into the world.

Sam completed his examination. "A bit undernourished, and I want to run some X-rays to make sure there's nothing internal. As long as those are clear, I think all this one needs is some intensive care days and she'll be good to go."

Eric watched as Hartwell tensed up a bit. "X-rays?

Overnight care? How much is that going to cost?" He wondered why she was worried about that as, from what he could tell, she and Branford were doing well.

He cleared his throat. "I can cover it, and you can pay me back."

Sam sent him a look, which he ignored. Hartwell rubbed her hand down her skirt. Other than clearing her face of makeup, she was still wearing the dress she'd been wearing this morning. He tried to ignore the effect the short skirt and miles of legs it revealed had on him.

"I can't let you do it."

Sam grinned. "If he pays, he gets a friend discount, which he can then pass on to you. We can also work on a payment plan if you need it. I always want to make sure the animals get the care they need."

Hartwell looked down into the box where the other puppies sounded like they were waking up from their naps. She blew out a breath. "Fine. I'll figure something out."

Sam examined the other puppies. The final verdict was that they all needed to be cleaned up, but other than the runt, they appeared perfectly healthy.

"It would be easier if you can foster them for a bit, and then I can arrange adoptions. I have a network, but we've had a puppy boom lately, and they're all filled up."

Hartwell's expression was definitely one of panic. "I've never had a dog. I don't know what to do."

"We'll give you some training. Believe me, you're a natural so far."

Eric touched her arm. "You'll be fine. Sam here hasn't let anyone take a dog home that he isn't completely sure is ready to care for it."

She blew out a breath and nodded. "And it's okay that I'm only temporary? I'm not sure that I can actually bring any of the dogs back with me to the city."

Eric rubbed his chest as he felt a weird pinch from the words.

Sam grinned at her. "You'll be fine. In fact, from my guess, I think these guys will be just ready to be adopted in a month, six weeks at most. Are you staying at the motel?"

"Yes. Is that a problem?"

"No. I'll just call Mrs. Keller and arrange for us to pay the pet fee. No reason you should take that on. I'll also get you sorted with some supplies for the puppies and the dog. Do you want to name her?"

"Um, I hadn't thought about it."

"Take your time. Let me know what you come up with and I'll make sure that whoever her next family is will be good with it. We don't need to get her used to one name, only to change it."

Orna came back into the room a few minutes later with the dog. Freshly cleaned, he could appreciate the gorgeous coat that had blended in well with the dirt and mud. She looked like she might be a cross between a husky and a chocolate lab.

Her attention went right to the box. Hartwell picked it up from the exam table and held it out for the dog to inspect. She apparently could tell that one was missing and began whining.

Sam immediately snapped his fingers, and she came to attention. "Up here." He moved the runt puppy up to the side of the exam table. The dog licked its little face, and it yipped in response.

"I'm going to keep her with me for a few days. You need to take care of the others. How's she doing, Orna?"

"In good condition. She's definitely the mom and is lactating. A few cuts, but that's to be expected with her being out in the woods. Everything seems to be healing okay, though."

"Any other injuries?"

"Not that I could tell."

"Chip?"

"Nope."

Sam growled. "I hate it when people don't properly care for their dogs."

Eric rocked back on his heels. Sam had always taken improper care of animals as a personal affront. "We've got her. We'll take her and the puppies and get on our way."

His friend nodded. "Yeah. Orna, can you get them set up with a foster kit? I'm going to put this little one in the incubation area to see if that'll help her, and then go examine Bacon. Also, Ms. Hartwell is going to need some training, as she's never fostered before."

"Okay." She smiled at Hartwell. "I'll go gather a kit for you and then come back and show you how it all works."

Hartwell mustered up a smile, but he could tell she was overwhelmed. "That would be great. Thank you."

When Sam and Orna left the room with the runt, he walked over and placed his hand on her shoulder. "You're doing good."

"I'm overwhelmed."

"Why? Didn't you have a dog when you were a kid?"

"No. My father didn't approve of them."

Eric scratched the back of his head. "Hunh. Well, did you want a puppy when you were a kid?"

"Kind of? I mean, don't most kids want a pet of some kind? I wasn't even allowed to have a fish."

He realized she still looked worried. "What's wrong?"

She blew out another breath and pet the dog's head. The dog leaned into her side, and he saw her shoulders relax a tiny bit. If she wasn't careful, this dog was going to adopt *her,* whether she was ready for it or not.

"We hadn't planned on me needing care for a dog, let alone puppies."

"We?"

"Me and Greer. I know she'll help me, but all this costs money."

"Yeah, pets are expensive. Even if you're only caring for them temporarily."

"If I could access my trust, that would be one thing. But I need to stay under the radar."

All his alarm bells pinged. "Stay under the radar? Why?"

She grimaced and dug her fingers into the dog's fur. "I ran away from my wedding." She looked at the nice watch she wore. "In fact, I was supposed to be getting married right now."

He took a step back. "You're a runaway bride?"

She shot him a look. "It's not contagious. You don't have to clean yourself of cooties or anything."

"What happened? Did he cheat on you?"

"No. I just realized that my father bought him for me."

He stood there, looking at her, trying to process what she'd said. "Bought him for you? I'm pretty sure that's completely immoral."

"In all the ways that could be taken. It seems that Herman's father has lost most of the family fortune and gone into debt because of a gambling addiction he's mostly been able to hide. My father offered to pay off those debts in exchange for controlling interest in the firm that they're partners in and Herman marrying me."

"Damn."

"Yep. Found out last night when I came home early from my bachelorette party to clean up after I had an entire tray of drinks dropped on me."

"Did you love him?"

"No. I mostly liked him, and I thought we had more in

common than we did. My father was at the apartment when I got home, but neither he nor Herman heard me come in. Herman was too busy yelling about how he was tired of this and wanted to tell me the truth. My father, being the upstanding person he is, threatened to send the loan sharks he'd bought the debts off of to the house to sit on Herman until the wedding. I slipped back out and called Greer to meet me at her place. Then I drove up here."

"Quite a night." Honestly, he was amazed that she seemed so in control of herself. He thought about what would have happened to Melody if she'd found herself in the same situation. And realized he'd probably be bailing her out of jail for assault, as she would have had both men by the balls.

Then he realized he had a golden opportunity. He cleared his throat. "Look. You need some extra cash, right?"

She looked up from the dog, whose eyes were closed and tongue lolling out the side of her mouth as Hartwell scratched the back of her neck. "I told you I had a job."

"And you also just told me you had a cash flow problem. I'll pay the vet bills and help out with any food you need for them."

"In exchange for what?"

"At least ten hours a week in my office getting things cleaned up and in order."

"But I'm supposed to be taking care of the puppies."

"You can bring them to the office. We'll make a puppy play area for when you're in the office."

She looked down at the dog. "He's really desperate, isn't he?"

The dog barked in apparent agreement.

"And you don't block us from becoming clients of the firm."

She shook her head. He thought that meant deal over. "I

already spoke to Greer and told her what happened. I'm sorry for doing that. It was unprofessional. I told her that if you still wanted to work with us, I fully supported it."

He was surprised, but he grunted an acknowledgement of the apology. "Accepted. Do we have a deal?"

She looked at the box and down at the dog again, before holding out a hand to him. "Deal."

He shook her hand to seal and, again, ignored the fire that tempted him to draw her closer. "Deal."

five

A WEEK LATER, LIBBY HAULED THE LITTLE WAGON SHE'D GOTTEN to carry the puppies around in through the door to Keller Builders. The dog, which she'd named Mayzie, followed in behind the wagon.

Melody ran around her desk. "Puppy Time!"

Libby laughed. "Where's your brother?"

"Still on his way in. He had a rough night."

Libby tried to not wonder hard about what had caused his hard night, but Eric had only marginally dialed back on the surliness. The other day, he asked her why she was still wearing her engagement ring.

"A. Because I don't want guys to hit on me. Not being engaged anymore doesn't mean that I'm looking for someone to date. And B. I don't want to lose the ring before I can give it back to Herman. It's not mine, and I'm sure it cost a lot of money."

He'd only grunted and turned his attention back to his computer.

Not even the puppies seemed to pull him out of his perpetual bad mood. He wasn't mean to them, but he also didn't go out of his way to cuddle with them the way Melody and everyone else they encountered did.

Even Greer had demanded hourly pictures of them and then had sent extra gift cards for things like the wagon.

Melody began pulling up the netting Libby used to keep the puppies in the wagon for now. The smallest puppy, Button, began trying to climb out. Libby gently pushed Button back into the wagon and pushed Melody out of the way. "You know the rules."

Melody looked up from where she knelt next to the wagon and did her best impression of Button, who was also staring up at her, pleading in her blue eyes.

"No. We're trying to train them the right way so they can be adopted out easily." Learning how to train puppies was something she'd never considered as a possibility in her life. Luckily, she'd been able to sign up for a temporary card with the public library and had gotten a bunch of dog care and training books. She'd even spent some of her precious gift cards on a super basic laptop so she could watch YouTube videos before bed.

"Button's mine."

"You keep saying that, but she still needs training and to stay in the puppy area while she's here."

Libby headed over to the corner where Eric had built puppy-safe fencing along with a gate for the wagon to pass through. She let all the puppies out of the wagon, and they started playing with each other and the toys that kept appearing each morning.

"Are you going to the job site today?"

Melody played tug with Button. "Yeah. We've got roofing and windows happening today. By the way, do you mind if Ana stops by later? She's been in a funk, and I told her she needs some puppy time."

"I'm good with that." Ana, the diner server who'd been

the one to push Libby into Eric's lap that first day, was Melody's best friend and would frequently drop by to chat for a bit between her shifts at the diner and the library.

"Great." Melody pulled her phone out of her pocket and started tapping away with one hand and pulling on the crackly cucumber that Button had claimed.

After checking on all her pups, Mayzie headed over to the dog bed Eric had added to the compound after the first day. Two of the puppies hurried over to get a snack.

Libby did a quick check, making sure she didn't have to replace any of the puppy pads, and then left the puppy area. The first few days she'd been here were spent trying to make heads or tails of what filing system the Kellers did have.

It amazed her they didn't fight more often considering how diametrically opposed they were in office management. Melody immediately cleared away all paper that fell into her areas. It was scanned and then shredded, or ended up in the recycling bin. Her problem was that her file naming convention only made sense to her.

The paper that fell into Eric's domain? Into the archaeological dig zone that was his desk. He claimed to know exactly where everything he needed was, but he also wasn't fighting about Operation Clean Eric's Desk.

Libby loved being a lawyer and contract negotiations, but she also had a secret fetish for organization videos and systems. When she and Greer had hired their office manager, she'd actually mourned having to give up her file management duties.

Since Melody was planning on being out of the office today, she'd work on sorting out the digital files once she left. Until then, she'd tackle Eric's desk.

She had cleared off about an inch of paper when the front door opened. She looked up and saw it was Ana.

Frowning, she checked her watch. As she suspected, the diner wasn't closed for the day yet.

As Ana came closer, she saw tear tracks on the other woman's cheeks. She called out to her temporary boss. "Melody."

"What?" Melody had gone into the back area a couple of minutes ago.

"Ana's here."

"What?" Libby heard some hurried movements, and then Melody rushed out of the back. "Ana? What happened?"

The dogs must have picked up on the emotional turmoil as they began yipping from the puppy area. Even Mayzie had her front paws on the top of the fencing.

Ana began crying. "My mom did it again."

Libby looked at Melody for guidance, but Melody ran over and engulfed Ana in a hug. "Do you need me to dig a grave?"

Ana's laugh was watery, but she did laugh. "No. Grams would prefer it if she didn't outlive any of her kids. Even the ones she's not particularly fond of."

Apparently, this was a frequent issue. Melody caught her gaze and shook her head while mouthing the words, "I'm gonna kill her one day."

"Come on, Ana Banana. It's Puppy Time."

The sound of the back door opening filtered through to them.

A minute later, Eric came through to the main office area. He looked first at Ana in Melody's embrace, and then at Libby, before going back to Melody and Ana. "Need me to get the backhoe?"

"No. I appreciate the sentiment, but you both need to knock it off in case something does happen to her one day."

Ana wiped her face and firmed her shoulders. "I need Puppy Time."

Melody took her over to the play area while Libby rooted around in Eric's drawers for tissues or something. He came over and placed the bags he was carrying on top of the paperwork she'd uncovered. "I've got it."

He picked up a pile on the floor she hadn't gotten to and revealed a box of industrial paper cloths.

"You can't give those to her."

He shrugged. "It's what we've got." He plucked two out of the box and went over to the puppy area. Mayzie tried to sniff what he was holding, and a few of the puppies thought they were a new plaything and jumped to nip at them.

Melody took them, keeping them out of the dogs' reach. "We've got roofing and windows at the Sullivans' today. I know you were going to work on paperwork, but can you handle that?"

"Sure." He looked over at Libby. "Mind coming with me?"

She blinked. "Why?"

"So you can meet the crew." He looked at her outfit. "You'll need to get changed first."

Recognizing from his tone that no would not be an acceptable answer, she thought over what she'd bought last week. "I don't have anything appropriate for being on a worksite."

"Do you have leggings? Close-toed shoes?"

"Yesssss..."

"Then you're fine. You won't be doing any of the work, just walking around part of the site. Let's go. Mel, I got lunch, so if you want it, go for it."

"Thanks. We'll have some intensive Puppy Time first."

Mayzie came over to the gate and whined. Melody

hooked a hand into the handle on her harness. "Sorry, Mayz, no dogs on site. You'll need to stay here."

Libby went over and pet Mayzie. "I promise I'll be back soon. Keep Melody and Ana company."

Mayzie whined once more, but eventually went over to Ana and licked her cheek.

Eric jangled his car keys by the back entrance. "Ready?"

"Yeah." She picked up her purse and followed him out the door.

He unlocked his truck by remote and waited as she climbed in. "Sorry about that. Ana's mom is the worst."

"Do you know what happened?"

He backed out of the parking spot and headed for the motel. "No, but this happens about once a month. Anything will set her off and then she takes it out on Ana."

"That sucks."

"Yep." He pulled into a spot at the motel near the office. "You go get changed, and I'll go in and let my mom know what happened."

"Okay." She hurried off to her room and quickly changed. Thanks to the dogs, pretty much everything, even the things she hadn't taken out of the bags yet, was covered in dog hair. They were damn cute, but it was a wonder they weren't bald from all the shedding they did.

She pulled out a pair of leggings and the tennis shoes she hadn't worn yet. Not the most supportive, but in her budget. She grabbed a couple of elastics to hold her hair back and then hurried back out to Eric's truck.

Eric was standing at the driver's side door, obviously in a heated conversation on the phone. He waved at her to get in, and she climbed into the truck.

Even though the soundproofing was good, she could still hear most of his side of the conversation. His last words were "Don't even think it."

He stood next to the truck, rubbing his forehead as if he had a headache. Libby reached over to knock on the window, but she only got close enough to brush her knuckles against the glass.

It was enough as he looked up at her. She watched as he rearranged his features to be not murderous. Still scowly, but he didn't immediately make her think of graves despite his earlier offer to Ana.

When he got in the truck and started it, he sat for a moment, staring at his hands.

"Are you okay?"

"I will be. Sorry about that."

She lifted one leg up so that her foot rested on the seat and waggled her foot. "Will these do?"

He stared at her leg and foot for a long while before he cleared his throat. "Yeah. Yeah, those will work. Like I said, it's not like you're actually going to be working."

He drove over to the job site. "The Sullivan project is a complete teardown and new build. One of their kids did well down on Wall Street and wanted to upgrade the family vacation home. The first floor has a master suite for the parents, entertainment room, and kitchen, with a deck off the back that leads to the lakefront."

"None of these houses look all that big."

"The lots aren't huge, but they're not ridiculously small. Plus, we've got some room to work with on depth as most of them have large back spaces on the lakefront."

The house that he drove them to was a couple miles from Sunflower Falls' downtown area.

"The other thing with the Sullivans is that the same kid who's financing this rebuild just bought the property next door, so if she likes what we do with this house, we're hoping she'll also hire us to do hers. And film it."

"What do you think your chances are?"

"Of getting the build contract? Good. We're known quantities here in Sunflower Falls. Filming? It's a toss-up. She likes her privacy." He pulled over on the road in front of the house.

It was two stories, and, from the front, didn't look much bigger than the older lake houses on either side. There were pallets of construction material sitting on the gravel drive that ran alongside the house. Workers were moving in and out of the house, a few of them wearing harnesses.

Eric reached into the backseat and pulled out a hard hat. "Stay here. I don't want you on site without a hat, and I don't have a spare with me in the truck. I'll be right back."

He climbed out and stuck the hat on his head. A hard hat should not stir feelings of desire, but it gave him an even more rugged look. She waved her hand in front of her face. "Chill down, Libby. You are a runaway bride and still need to deal with the consequences of that."

She pulled out her phone and texted Greer to see what the latest with Herman and her father was. Apparently, Herman had also headed out of town. Her father was still checking in with Greer to find out where she was. He'd also confirmed that he was monitoring her credit cards and other accounts, so she was stuck with using the gift cards Greer was sending.

Libby hated that Eric had been right about the cash issue because Melody had paid her yesterday for her hours, and having that cushion had soothed an anxiety she hadn't even realized she'd been feeling until it was gone.

She watched as he ran over to one of the workers. The person went to a truck parked in the driveway and pulled out a black hard hat. Eric took it and jogged back over to her.

Climbing out of the truck, she held out a hand to him. He gave her the hard hat. She put it on, and it immediately slipped down over her eyes. "Do you have something smaller?"

"Turn around."

She did. He adjusted the hat, so it sat level on her head, and then did something at the back. She felt the inner parts of the hat tightening on her head. As soon as they started to feel pinchy, she spoke up. "That's good."

He came around and wiggled the brim. When it barely moved, he nodded. "Keep that on. When we're done here, I'll return it to Donna."

He started walking away, so she hurried to keep pace with him. The front yard was ripped to shreds and was primarily small patches of grass peeking through the dirt. Eric raised a hand to the person he'd gotten the hard hat from. "Donna, this is Libby Hartwell. She's working at the office part time to help deal with the paperwork. Libby, this is Donna Hernandez, our on-site foreperson."

The woman looked Libby up and down. "At least you're not wearing sandals."

Libby held out a hand. "These were the best I had for what Eric told me to wear."

Donna shook her hand, and Libby felt the calluses left by years of hard, manual labor. "Did you just move to Sunflower Falls?"

"Kind of. I'm here just for a month or so."

"Really? And hard ass over here hired you?" Donna looked at Eric, who was scratching the back of his neck, avoiding her gaze.

"Melody hired her. Mostly."

Donna pulled her phone out of her back pocket. "And where is Melody? She was supposed to approve the shingles and windows before we started installation."

"Ana's mom did something, so Ana's over at the office. Puppy therapy, I guess."

Donna grinned and shot a quick glance over at Libby. "I heard there was an influx of puppies. I'll have to stop by the office sometime and see them."

Libby smiled. "I'm usually there on Tuesdays, Thursdays, and Saturdays."

"Perfect. Now, about these shingles and windows. We need to get them in today if we're going to keep to schedule."

They walked over to the pallets, and Eric took a couple pictures which he sent to Melody. He then checked the labeling on the pallets against something on his phone. Libby heard a ding, and Eric grinned. "We're good to go. As long as they didn't slip in the odd mismatch, Melody says this is what she ordered."

Libby watched as workers swarmed the piles and began disassembling them. Seeing the efficient way the workers went about their jobs distracted her, so when she caught sight of Eric again, she was surprised to see him wearing a harness, too.

"What are you doing?"

He jerked his thumb in the direction of a lift. "Going up on the roof. The first day of roofing, we have a contest to see who can lay the most amount of shingles. Whoever wins has to buy the beer for the next company party."

She looked up at the roof and swallowed. It was only twenty or so feet off the ground, but you were in the air. With nothing to catch you. "You're..." she cleared her throat. "You're going up?"

"Yeah. Why?"

"I thought you were going to show me around or something. Inside."

His eyes narrowed as he began buckling the harness closed and tightening the straps. "Are you afraid of heights or something?"

"Yes." She'd never liked being up high and even hated seeing people in places where there weren't obvious barriers to them taking a flying leap, even an unintentional one, off wherever they were.

He placed his hands on her shoulders, but when she refused to meet his gaze, he tipped her chin up with a finger. "Hartwell, look at me. We follow the highest safety practices. I care about my crew and I'd be a shit boss if I didn't model what I require. None of us are going to fall off."

"But if you're working fast, you won't be paying close attention."

He grinned. "That's the best part about this contest. You can't cut any corners. Everything has to be laid better than code and you have to be fully strapped into a harness at all times. The constrictions make the contest more fun."

She blew out a breath. "Fine. How long does it last?"

"At least an hour. Depends on when I need to head home or to the office."

"Okay. I can last an hour." She hoped.

Eric headed over to the lift with two of the other workers, and Donna was the operator. Once they were on the roof and confirmed they were attached to the safety system, Donna lowered the lift and locked it down.

She came over to where Libby stood. "You okay?"

Libby lifted a shoulder. "I'll have to be, won't I?"

"Eric's good. He doesn't allow anyone fucking around. If they do, they get two warnings to shape up. If they don't, they're fired."

"He's a good boss?"

"The best. We're really hoping that he and Melody can get the show deal."

Libby tore her gaze away from where Eric and the

workers were beginning the process of laying the shingles and looked at Donna. "Why?"

"Because he and Melody were good on their uncle's show, and it'll help bring some attention to Sunflower Falls. The town's been working to improve the job situation around here, but we've got a lot of kids heading out for better opportunities. I want my kids to actually have the option to stay if they want."

"Knock, knock."

They both turned around, and Libby saw the two men who'd been the targets of Ana's accident with her tray last week. She'd seen both of them around town while walking Mayzie.

She smiled and saw that Donna was frowning at them. "Zach Troy. I'd heard you were back in town. What are you doing here? Isn't your parents' place on the other side of town?"

The one with reddish brown hair and who'd ended up wearing most of the food scowled. "Hey, Donna. We're just walking around."

She crossed her arms. "Who's your friend?"

Mr. Smiley grinned at both of them and held out a hand to Donna. "Tony Caputo. Nice to meet you."

Donna looked at the hand, and Libby saw her brows raise, but she shook his hand. "This is a construction site. You can't be here without hard hats."

Mr. Smiley, Caputo, turned to Libby and winked. "Do you have any extras? I'd love to see what you're doing with this place."

Libby saw his friend, Zach, roll his eyes. "Tony here is thinking he might like to buy a place on the lake and build new. How about it, Donna?"

Donna looked to Libby, and then up at the roof. "Sure. I

guess. Libby, why don't you come with us, and I'll give you all a walkthrough."

Donna got hard hats for the men, and once they were properly outfitted, led the way into the house. Before going inside, Libby looked up and caught Eric staring at them. As usual, he was scowling. She wondered what had gotten him all knotted up this time around and then headed in. Caputo was waiting for her and held out an elbow to her. There was something in the gesture that rang bells in the back of her mind. "I missed your name last week. I'd love the name of the woman with the gorgeous dog."

She couldn't help but smile up at him. "Libby Hartwell. Nice to meet you. Does anyone ever tell you that you look familiar?"

He blinked, as if startled, and then grinned even harder. Almost as if he was forcing it the tiniest bit. "I've got doppelgangers all over the world."

six

Eric stared down at where Donna had led Hartwell, Zach, and his friend into the house.

"Hey, boss. What's got you riled up? You're going to lose." Mike didn't even pause in swinging his hammer to tack in the nails securing the shingles to the roof.

He yanked his attention back to the job at hand. "Nothing."

"Looking at Zach's pretty boy friend? Anyone know what his deal is?" Patty kept the same rhythm as Mike. Which made sense, as they'd been teamed up for roofing over the last two years.

Eric just grunted and hoped they'd move on with the conversation. He didn't want to dwell on Zach's friend or what he may be doing with Hartwell in the house. Not that it was likely to be much with Donna and Zach there. Especially as all that was there was framing and subflooring.

Mike sliced open another pack of shingles. This pack would be his third, about the same as Patty, while Eric was a little behind thanks to the distraction. He tried to block his crew out as he focused on catching up and getting ahead.

"Rumor I heard is that he met up with Zach in the Marines, and they got back in touch when Zach was in Hollywood. Doesn't seem much like a Marine. At least, not like Zach is totally a Marine."

Out of the corner of his eye, Eric saw Patty sit back on her heels. "No way that man is a Marine. He's way too pretty."

Mike pointed his hammer at Patty. "If women can be, and are, Marines, that means pretty boys can also be Marines."

"He looks so familiar, but I can't place why. I know I've seen him before."

Eric grunted. "I thought we were supposed to be having a contest here. Not talking about people wandering the worksite."

Patty resumed laying her stack of shingles. "That's another thing. What's Donna doing taking them into the house? I mean, I understand your friend, Eric, but why Zach and his friend? What's her name again?"

"Hartwell. Libby Hartwell." He tried to make it as matter of fact as possible, but he could hear how his tone softened the tiniest bit when he said her first name. Which was why he tried to only refer to her by her last name, even in his head. It helped keep some distance.

Which she said she wanted when she told him why she still wore her engagement ring. Not that he'd hook up with anyone not ready to completely cut ties with a former boyfriend, fiancè, whatever. The fact she was wearing her ring should have reassured him about her handling Zach's friend, but he got the impression that Zach's friend wouldn't let a thing like a ring get in his way.

Feeling frustration rise in his gut, he channeled it into his arm and proceeded to get ahead of both Mike and Patty.

When Donna reappeared below and called time, he'd

laid four and a half packs of shingles, with Mike and Donna just opening their fifth pack.

Patty wiped her forehead with the bandana she kept in her back pocket. "Good job, boss. I'm looking forward to shandy at the company picnic."

"Noted. What about you, Mike?"

"The usual."

Eric groaned. "When are you going to take advantage of me and ask for the good stuff?"

"Miller Lite is perfectly good."

"If you're a teenager from Chicago with no damn money."

Mike crossed his arms against his chest. "I was a teenager from Chicago with no damn money. I like it."

Patty slapped his back. "At least he's not asking for Malort."

Eric choked down a bark of laughter. Last year, for their winter Ice Party, Mike had brought a couple bottles of what he'd declared was a little-known Chicago tradition and had everyone who chose to drink alcohol take a shot. Two of the guys had ended up gagging and throwing it back up.

At that moment, Donna parked the lift on the roof. They unhooked their safety lines and climbed onto the lift. The ride down to ground level felt like it took forever as he watched Hartwell talking with Zach and his friend. The other guy was all up in Hartwell's space, but she didn't seem to do anything to discourage him.

When the lift was back on the ground, he was first out and walked over to the group. Not even thinking, he threw an arm around Hartwell's shoulders.

"We should get back to the office."

The look she threw in his direction was absolute shock and horror.

"Excuse me?" She took hold of his hand and shoved his arm off her. As she should.

The second his skin touched hers, he knew he had to back off. But that knowing warred with the feeling that he had to stake his claim in front of Zach and his friend.

Zach rubbed his mouth, and Eric had the feeling his former friend was trying to hide a smile. Zach's friend wasn't even bothering.

He held out his hand to Eric. "Tony Caputo. Nice to meet you, officially, and without food all over me. Though it was mostly all over Troy here."

Eric let the other man's chill wash over him and relaxed a bit. Hartwell turned on her heel and walked over to Donna.

He watched her until he heard Zach cough. Turning back, he caught Caputo smiling again. Eric stared at him, and Caputo raised his hands. "I get the message. Besides, she's giving off all the not interested vibes. I don't go where I'm not wanted."

"Good."

"Eric, Tony's interested in possibly buying a property here as a teardown. I told him you'd be the best person to talk to."

Eric looked at Zach. "What about your mom? She's the real estate agent around here."

Caputo stuck his hands in his back pocket. "I talked with Mrs. Troy. She gave me a list of properties, but I wanted an opinion on what would need to be done to meet my vision. If a full tear down is needed, or just renovations, and which is more cost efficient."

Eric looked at Zach again, who nodded. "Which properties are you looking at?"

Caputo named a few properties which were on the part of the lake where the lots were larger. He then talked about what he was looking to get out of the rebuilds. It was some serious money for Sunflower Falls. Even considering his current project. "I'll have to check with my sister. She's the lead designer for projects like this, and would need to be on hand for the walkthroughs."

Caputo grinned. "Great. When can we arrange this? I want to get moving as soon as possible. At least to purchase the property. I don't want my top pick to get snatched out from under me."

"What about financing?" Most of the homeowners they worked with had to arrange for additional financing one way or another to get the project to the level they wanted.

"It'll be an all-cash deal." This time, it was Caputo who looked over at Zach, and Eric couldn't quite put his finger on what bothered him about it. "I've had a couple of good investments over the years, and I'm looking to move into real estate. I'm not likely to be here full time, but I'd like a place comfortable enough for friends to use when they need to get away from things."

Eric frowned, but he caught the slight shake of Zach's head and decided he didn't want to know. He knew Zach had gone into the private protection thing when he left the Marines, so Caputo might be a client of some kind. "I'll check with Melody once we get back to the office. What's your number or email so I can contact you?"

He pulled a notepad out of the pocket of his work shirt and jotted down the number and email that Caputo gave him.

Caputo held out a hand. "Thanks, man. I really appreciate this. I have a question, though."

"Yeah?"

"Eric and Melody? Like Eric Braeden and Melody Thomas Scott?"

"The fuck?" No one had ever connected how he and

Melody had gotten their names. At least, not since they were adults and people rarely had access to their middle names. No way did he ever want people to know he and his sister had been named after his mom's favorite soap opera couple.

Caputo shrugged. "It's a gift. I see connections where others don't always and it gets me into trouble sometimes. Believe me, I won't say anything."

Zach was frowning. "What am I missing?"

Eric rubbed his face. "Melody and I are named after Mom's favorite soap couple."

"Okay." He drew out the word and then shook his head. "Hey, do you want to meet us for drinks over at Geraghty's later? Around six?"

"Sure." A flash of bright blue caught his attention, and he looked over to see Hartwell headed back to them. As she made her way over the uneven ground, he thought back to when she showed off the shoes he had on. He had to purge his mind of thoughts of how else she could put her flexible legs to use. Preferably around his head.

That required another scrub of the face, as he couldn't rearrange his dick without calling attention to it.

She kept her attention on Eric. "Can you give me a lift back to the office? I need to take the puppies home."

"Sure."

"Puppies? I love puppies." Of course Caputo loved puppies.

She glanced at him. "Yes. I'm fostering a dog and her puppies until they can be adopted out."

Eric had a strong feeling that Mayzie wouldn't be adopted out to anyone. Hartwell may not see it yet, but that dog had decided that she was her human.

Before Caputo could say anything more, he took hold of Hartwell's arm and led her back to the truck. He took the hard hat from her and made sure she was secure in the truck before he ran it back to Donna.

"Bring her back any time, boss. She's not annoying like some of the other women who've tried to date you."

"She's not trying to date me."

"Which is why I don't find her as annoying. But you are definitely interested in her."

Considering he did his absolute best not to lie to his crew about anything, he swallowed the instinctive denial. Protecting himself wouldn't help ensure he had the total and complete trust of those he worked with.

Donna laughed and slapped him on the back. "Get out of here. And tell Melody to call me."

"Will do."

He jogged back to the truck as Zach and Caputo were coming over to return their hard hats.

"Eric. Wait up."

Zach tossed his hat to Donna and then came over to him. "Geraghty's at six?"

"Sure."

He pulled out his phone. "Give me your number in case something comes up."

Eric recited his number and Zach quickly typed it in. He then did something and Eric felt his phone vibrate as a message came in. "That was so you've got mine for the same reason."

"Thanks. See you later."

Zach gave him a small salute and walked back over to Caputo. Eric climbed into the driver's seat and glanced at Hartwell. "They treat you okay?"

She looked back at him with one brow raised. "Better than you. What was with that caveman display?"

"Nothing."

"You have never touched me like that. Do not tell me it was nothing."

To give himself some mental space before replying, he checked traffic and pulled out onto the road. She gave him until they were a couple of blocks from the Sullivan site. "I'm still waiting."

He blew out a breath. "I'm not sure."

"Eric."

"Yeah, I know. That's not a good answer. I know it's a shit answer. But it's all I got. When I saw Caputo trying to make nice with you, I'm not sure what came over me."

"Tony's nice. Yes, he was flirting, but I get the impression that he flirts with every woman he sees. Frankly, I think he just flirts with everyone with little intention of it being sexual. That man loves people."

He let that tumble around in his mind as he drove back through town. She wasn't wrong. Caputo seemed to enjoy making connections with people. He wondered what his deal was. Maybe he could find out more tonight. He also knew he needed to apologize to Hartwell for what she called the caveman display. "I'm sorry."

"Thank you. And I apologize for being so anxious about you being up on the roof."

He glanced at her. "Why? It's anxiety. You can't control that."

She chewed on her lip, which sent his thoughts in other directions they really shouldn't be traveling. "Just because I have anxiety doesn't mean I need to place that worry on others. Particularly the person I'm worried about who's about to climb up on a roof."

He turned down the alley that led to the back entrance of the office. "Okay, fine. But it's still not anything to be sorry about. Going up on roofs is what I do, but I respect that you've got issues around that. It'd be like me apologizing for having brown hair or being a lefty."

She laughed, but he heard a watery tone to it, and he turned to her after he put the truck in park. Hartwell was scrubbing her face. "What now?"

She blew out a long breath. "Thank you. Having anxieties about things is not acceptable in Hartwells, even when taking my gender into account."

He waited until she met his gaze. "For the record..." He trailed off, not sure if he really should say it to her.

She tilted her head. "Yes?"

Well, it wasn't like he was ever going to meet her father. "Your father is a Grade A dick. And I say that with also having a father who created the standard for Grade A dicks."

She laughed and then leaned over the console and gave him a hard hug. "Thank you."

He watched as she climbed out of the truck and headed into the office. The sheer joy on her face was amazing.

And he was sitting in his truck because he'd gotten a boner so fast it rivaled when he was in high school and the cheerleaders would walk past him in the hall.

Eric banged his head against the headrest. "Why? Why me?"

Melody popped her head out of the back door. "You okay?"

"Give me a minute."

She walked over to his door and crossed her arms against the open window. She rested her chin on them. "You win the roofing contest?"

"Yeah. Four and a half packs to about four for both Mike and Patty."

She held up a fist, and he bumped it. "Dad call?"

He scowled at her. "How the hell did you know?"

"Because the asshole tried to call both me and Mom. I let it go to voicemail and haven't listened to it yet. Mom texted me the gist of what he's trying to sell."

And with that, his boner disappeared. Now he knew what he needed to think of any time it acted up around Hartwell. His own Grade A Dick father.

Melody patted his shoulder. "You need to block him, Eric. He's not worth it."

"That's what Mom says, too."

"So listen to her. If Uncle Stef was in town, he'd kick Dad's ass out of the county."

"Which is why he's here. He knows Stef's not around."

Melody grinned at him. "Aren't you glad we have a much healthier sibling relationship?"

He laughed. "We definitely got lucky, despite who Mom named us after."

She curled her lips. "What the hell brought that up?"

"I met a guy at the site today. Tony Caputo. He's a friend of Zach Troy's, and when I mentioned your name as my sister, he apparently immediately pegged who we were named after."

Melody frowned. "So weird."

"Yeah."

She stepped back so he could get out of the truck. "Why were they at the site?"

"Caputo wants to buy property here and either tear down what's there and build new or remodel. He wants our input on the best property and what the best solution would be for that property."

"Why not go through Mrs. Troy?"

"He's already asked her, and she's given him a short list."

Melody scratched the back of her right wrist. "That

could be interesting. If we can't get Nora to let us film the build of her property, maybe we can convince him."

"I'll let you deal with that. He annoys me." He followed her back into the office.

She glanced over her shoulder and grinned at him. "Was he flirting with Libby?"

When she tripped over something on the floor, he reached out and steadied her even as he rolled his eyes. "Leave it, Melody."

"Shhhhh."

They both looked up to find Hartwell holding her finger up to her lips.

Eric made sure his voice was low when he asked his question. "The puppies?"

"And Ana."

"What?" Melody pushed past Hartwell and stared down at the puppy play area. She had her fist on her hips and shook her head.

He looked at Hartwell. "She only came out a couple of minutes ago. What happened to Ana?"

Hartwell was grinning. "Come see."

She reached out and grabbed his wrist to pull him into the office area. As soon as he cleared the doorway, he saw. Ana was sprawled out on the floor, fast asleep, with all the puppies piled on top of her, also asleep. Mayzie was on the dog bed in the corner. She looked over at them and let out a low woof.

None of them wanted to disturb the quiet, so they went about their business as soundlessly as possible. After Melody took probably a hundred photos on her phone.

Eric checked his watch. He had a few hours before he had to meet Zach and Caputo at Geraghty's. He texted Melody his plans for the evening. When it hit her phone, she read it, looked up at him, and then did a very exaggerated, but silent, chair dance.

She then began furiously texting away on her phone, but he saw it was Hartwell she was messaging when she pulled her phone out.

He wasn't about to get in the middle of them, so he went back to work answering emails he couldn't put off any longer. Branford had sent over a representation contract for him to review with Melody. He forwarded that to their attorney to check it over for anything glaring.

Once he'd taken care of that, he tagged a few more emails for forwarding to Branford as soon as they came to an agreement. The production company they had been in talks with would also need to be notified about the change in representation. They were decent people, and he'd felt that they were straight shooters, but it never hurt to be as covered as possible.

There was a commotion in the puppy play area, and he looked over to see Ana sitting up with the puppies tumbling off her.

"Where am I?"

"In Puppy Play Land, Sleeping Beauty. Get yourself home and go get ready for a night out." Melody snapped her fingers in the air.

"What?" Ana had slept over at their house often enough when they were kids he was used to her complete incoherency when waking up. It was somehow even worse when someone else woke her up.

Hartwell got up and went over to the gate. Instead of risking puppies getting loose, she climbed over it, then helped Ana stand up.

"You okay?"

"She's fine. It takes her brain about ten minutes to wake up after her body does. You get the puppies together and head back to the motel. I already texted Mom, and she's happy to puppy and dog sit tonight, so no excuses."

Eric kept his head down so he wouldn't get sucked into his sister's organizational chaos. He was too late. She pointed at him. "And none of you testosterone types get any ideas to go anywhere besides Geraghty's tonight."

He held up his hands. "I wouldn't dream of it."

"Better not. Libby, go shopping if you need to. We are going to do it up tonight. It's been forever since I've had a girls' night out, and Ana here is in dire need of one."

"The puppies..."

"Give them to my mom earlier if you need to. I promise she'll love it, even if Maxwell doesn't."

Hartwell chewed her lip, giving him ideas all over again.

She finally blew out a breath. "Sure. It can't be worse than my bachelorette party last week."

Eric rubbed the back of his neck. Suddenly, a girls' night out sounded like a recipe for disaster. He wondered if he should expect a call at some point tonight to bail the three of them out.

seven

LIBBY HANDED MAYZIE'S LEASH OVER TO MRS. KELLER. "I'VE GOT backups of everything in my room, so if you need anything, you can grab it from there. It's all in a box that's sitting on the table so they can't get into it."

Mrs. Keller looked up from where she was petting Mayzie. "They'll be perfectly fine with me. I don't have grandkids I can spoil, so I'm going to take the next best opportunity."

Libby didn't want to go anywhere near a conversation about why Mrs. Keller didn't have grandkids. It was not any of her business. None at all why Eric was still single. She knew why Melody was still single. Because Melody had no problems sharing that she had yet to meet a man worthy of her.

Eric though? That man was wound so tight that he was in danger of snapping. She'd resisted looking up old episodes of To the Bones, but she hoped he managed some kind of on-camera charisma, otherwise her and Greer's signing of the siblings would be a disaster.

Mayzie looked up at her with the saddest gaze. She bent down and rubbed the spot on the back of Mayzie's neck that she'd discovered the dog liked best. "You'll be fine with Mrs. Keller. I'll be home later tonight. I promise."

Mayzie leaned against her, but didn't bark or anything as Libby left the motel's front office. Progress. The dog really didn't like it when Libby even stepped out of the room without her. Libby would have to figure out how to train her for adoption.

As she was opening the door to her room, Melody's SUV pulled into the lot. Melody leaned out the window. "Forget going out for new clothes. You're close enough to Ana's sister that we can raid her closet. Get your purse and get down here."

Libby wanted to argue, but Melody was a lot like Greer in that once she'd decided on a course of action, there was no stopping her. Instead, she waved and went into her room to grab her purse and a change of underwear. She also tossed the most necessary toiletries into a small bag she'd picked up. She still hadn't been able to shower after visiting the Sullivan site earlier, and no way was she going out without cleaning the construction dust from her body.

When she got down to the parking lot, Melody was tapping out a tune on her door. Melody grinned at her. "Ready? Ana's going to meet us at my place after she gets some clothes options from her sister."

Libby climbed into the passenger seat. "I should do something to thank her, right?"

Melody shook her head. "She should thank you. Ana's sister collects clothes and never wears them out. She's got two toddlers with a third kid on the way. Her husband works for the wind turbine plant an hour away, so when she gets dressed up, she gets as far as dropping off the kids with family and then they're on each other in the bedroom."

Melody drove her to a small house nestled in a little

neighborhood that led into the woods where Sunflower Falls got its name. A small sedan was already parked in front of it.

"Excellent. Ana's already here, so we don't have to waste any time. Hopefully, she's already in the shower because I've only got one bathroom."

"I should have made you wait while I showered in my room."

"Nope. No wasting time here." Melody walked around to the front door and opened it. Libby followed, a little unsure of herself. "Ana, we're back. Get moving because we've got a line going."

Libby looked around. From the outside, the house appeared well-tended, but in line with its neighbors. Inside, though, was an explosion of color and texture. Melody had filled the living room with rainbows and cozy clouds. It led into a kitchen that could use a facelift, but everything was sparkling clean and nothing out of place. In one corner between the counters and the eating area was a stand with a rainbow of pots on each shelf.

"Have a seat on the couch. Don't worry about the blankets, they're washable. Once Ana's out of the shower, you can hop in. It'll take me only five minutes to get ready once you're done."

Libby shook her head. This small house was more welcoming and lived in than the apartment her father had commissioned a professional decorator to fill and arrange for her. Supposedly as her law school graduation gift. The first thing she needed to do when she got back to the city was move out of there. It would never be her home.

Ana stuck her head out of a door that looked like it led to the private area of Melody's home. "I was wondering what was causing all this noise. Hi, Libby. You can have the

79

bathroom in a moment. Melody, grab me a glass of chardonnay, please."

Melody grinned at Libby. "There's a reason we're best friends."

Twenty minutes later, Libby was holding her own glass of chardonnay as she surveyed the options Ana had laid out on Melody's bed.

"You're sure your sister doesn't mind me borrowing her clothes?"

Ana laughed. "She practically threw them at me. She also said that whatever you picked, you could have. I didn't know what size shoe you wore, so I don't have any options for that."

Libby gave thanks she'd thrown in a pair of black flats to her bag. She'd debated getting them at the store, but figured they were a reasonable shoe option no matter the outfit.

She looked at the dresses. Every single one of them could have been what she'd worn to her bachelorette party. In fact, if she hadn't thrown away the dress in a fit of not wanting to be reminded of the night, she could have worn it out tonight.

Melody came out of the bathroom. "Still debating?"

"Yes. I'm not really sure if this is the right thing for me to do. I wore something similar to my bachelorette party just last week."

Melody grinned. "All the more reason for you to go out and let your hair down."

Ana chewed on her thumbnail and looked between the two of them. "Melody, if Libby doesn't feel like going out, we can just stay here. I'm good with that."

Melody's features grew firm. "Look, we all need to go out. Libby, it's not like you'll be reliving whatever happened at your bachelorette party. Ana, you need to realize there's life outside of this town."

Ana frowned, but before she could say something, Melody held her hand up. "Eric, Zach, and Zach's friend are going to be at Geraghty's. If they hadn't already claimed it, I'd just take the both of you over there and we could get drunk on decent beer and good food. But we do not need to deal with men we know. We need new men who we'll never see again if we don't want to."

Libby bit down on her lips to hide her smile. Melody sounded like she was prepping the high school team she coached to go out onto the field and win the game. She even ended her speech by pounding her fist into the palm of her other hand.

Ana caught her gaze and rolled her eyes.

Melody pointed at the both of them, wagging her finger between their faces. "I see the two of you. Don't tell me you don't need a break. Libby, I get that you being here is a break from your real life, but I'm sure you need a break from my big brother and not having any change of scenery."

Realizing it would be absolutely useless to argue with Melody, Libby held up her hands. "Fine. I'll go wherever you take me."

"Ana?"

"Okay. Yes. I could use a night out where I don't run the chance of running into my mother."

Melody shot both fists into the air. "Victory! Libby, you put on that green dress."

While Melody rooted around in her walk-in closet, Libby took the dress—the least showy of the options—into the bathroom, and got changed. The fabric had a lovely drape, and she felt a bit more confident in herself.

There was a bang on the door that connected the bathroom to Melody's bedroom. "Let's get going. I don't want to miss happy hour."

An hour later, they were at a club in the nearest big town. Libby didn't have a small purse, so Ana held on to her phone, ID, and the cash she'd brought with.

They sat at a table in a corner sharing a couple of appetizers as the DJ played some of the latest dance hits. It was still early enough that the dance floor wasn't overly crowded, but there were enough other people Libby wasn't sure if she wanted to get out there.

"Didn't I tell him to not leave Geraghty's?"

The near shout from Melody had Libby dropping the chip and dip she'd grabbed. She tried to look over Melody's shoulder, but she was just enough shorter than the other woman that she couldn't make out much besides the dance floor. Melody slid out of her seat and stalked over to the bar.

Libby leaned over to Ana. "What's going on?"

Ana was digging around in her purse. "I can't see."

Melody had volunteered to be the designated driver, partially because Ana had trouble with night driving, and she wasn't sure what Libby's tolerance was.

"I thought you were wearing contacts."

Ana blinked. "Oh. Yeah. I am." She turned in her seat and squinted over at where Melody was in some guy's face.

It took her a moment to realize it was Eric. The guys he was supposed to be out with were next to him at the bar. Tony was looking at Melody like she was the finest entertainment.

"Didn't he promise to stay at...wherever they were going?"

"Geraghty's. It's the closest thing Sunflower Falls has to a night life. And, yeah." Ana frowned, but didn't seem inclined to do anything.

"Should we go over there?"

She vehemently shook her head. "I don't want to set Melody off any more than she is." Ana grinned at her. "You might have noticed by now that Melody can be a bit dramatic."

Libby laughed. "Yeah, I noticed."

It was interesting that she didn't mind watching Melody's antics, as long as she wasn't also caught in the spotlight. Greer was good at commanding attention when she wanted it, but Melody demanded attention when she was in the mood.

At that moment, Melody did a literal flounce and began making her way back to the table. Libby saw Eric roll his eyes and turn to the bar. But before he got there, Tony had hooked his arm and began pulling him to where they were sitting.

When Melody plopped down on her chair, Ana picked up her drink and sucked on the straw. Leaving Libby to be the one to break the news. She cleared her throat, and when she had Melody's attention, she pointed behind her.

Melody turned just in time to have Tony standing behind her and Eric shoved in the general direction of Libby. Zach was casually strolling in their direction despite obvious looks sent his way.

"I told you this was a girls' night out. Go away." She made a shooing motion with her hands.

Eric leaned against the wall next to Libby and pointed at Tony. "Talk to him. I just wanted a beer."

Libby looked up at him. "What happened to Geraghty's?"

He smiled down at her. "There was a water main break, so all the businesses served by it had to shut down."

Libby winced. "I'm sorry."

"Again, not your fault. Stop apologizing for things you can't control."

Libby opened her mouth to say...something, but Eric stared at her, daring her to come up with some kind of rational response. And she couldn't. He was right. She was totally in the habit of apologizing for things that weren't in any way in her control. Because her father had trained her to do exactly that. Any time he was mad about something, and she was present, she apologized.

The bar association lost his response for some gala dinner? She apologized.

A judge's decision favored the other party? She apologized.

The housekeeper wasn't able to get his favorite brand of scotch? She apologized.

He never once said it wasn't her fault.

A club with thumping music playing through the speakers was not the best environment for a realization like this.

She wanted to talk with Greer.

"Ana, can I have my phone?"

Ana looked a little surprised, but extracted the phone from her purse and passed it over.

"Excuse me."

Eric placed his hand on her shoulder, and she realized thanks to the warmth of it how cold she'd gotten. "Are you okay?"

"Yeah. I just need some fresh air."

She headed for the exit, and it was only once she was outside that she realized he had followed her. "What? I need to make a phone call."

"You don't look like you're okay. Do I need to apologize?"

She shook her head. "You weren't wrong. It was...it

just...brought up stuff. I'm going to call Greer." She held up the phone, but before she could do anything more, a couple of the bouncers tossed out a guy who immediately stumbled into Libby.

The impact knocked her off balance, and as she tried to catch herself, her phone went flying. Eric grabbed her to him, and he twisted his body so that he was between her and the guy.

A distant crunching sound made her wince.

"Fuck off, you assholes. And fuck you, too."

Eric jerked, and Libby completely lost her footing. She scrambled to right herself, but her feet got tangled up in Eric's. They started going down, and Eric rolled.

They hit the ground. She could hear scuffling happening behind them. Her only worry was Eric, as he once again put himself between her and danger.

She pushed up her hands against the firm muscles of his chest. They were in a pocket of shadow, so she couldn't tell how badly he might be hurt.

"Eric?" She ran her hands over his upper body, and could feel his muscles clenching as if still trying to absorb the impact. "Are you okay? Do you need an ambulance?"

A bright light came over her shoulder, and Eric held his hand up to block it. "Watch it."

"You okay, man? You went down pretty hard. Sorry about that."

Libby looked over her shoulder and made out one of the bouncers. "I think he needs an ambulance."

"I don't need an ambulance."

She looked back down at him. "Did you hit your head? If you hit your head, you need to be checked out. No matter what, you need to be checked. You got injured because of actions of the employees and their insurance is going to want to have you checked."

"I'm not..."

She slapped her hand over his mouth to stop the words. "Do not. I'm your legal representative."

"Shit. You're a lawyer?"

"Yes. Please call an ambulance."

"Sure." The light disappeared with the bouncer, so she couldn't make out Eric's look, but she felt him glaring.

"Stop it. You know you should get checked."

"I didn't hit my head."

She crossed her arms against her chest. "Are you sure? You could have bounced that hard head against the concrete and never even noticed."

"Do you mind getting off me?"

"What?"

He closed his eyes and lowered his head to the ground. "Please. Get. Off. Me."

She realized she was straddling him, and there was some intriguing action happening against her ass. She scrambled off.

He curled up into a sitting position and groaned, one hand going to the back of his head.

"I told you. You need to go to the hospital."

"Listen, I've had my brains scrambled before. I don't have a concussion. Just a sore spot on the back of my head."

Just then, the rest of their party came spilling out the door.

"What the fuck, Eric? You can't go one weekend without getting into a fight?"

He glared up at his sister for a moment, and then winced. "I did not get into a fight. I was trying to avoid one."

Zach crouched down by him and turned on the flashlight on his phone, shining the light in Eric's eyes. "Your pupils look normal. Why did we leave Geraghty's?"

"Water main break."

"Any fogginess?"

"No."

"How many of me do you see?"

"Just the one."

"Feeling like you can stand?"

"Maybe."

Zach stood up and held a hand out to Eric. He reached up and clasped Zach's wrist. When he got to his feet, he was a bit wobbly, but steadied after a minute with Zach's hand on his shoulder. When Zach stepped away, they all waited for him to fall, but he was firm in his stance.

"I'm good."

By this time, the manager had come out and was dealing with both the belligerent drunk who was yelling for his own lawyer and their group.

A fire truck and an ambulance arrived soon after, with the cops pulling in after them. The medics checked out Eric and confirmed that it didn't appear he had a concussion, but recommended getting checked out by his own doctor tomorrow if he wouldn't go to the hospital.

"I'll make the call."

Melody was glaring at the drunk guy, who was still sitting on the ground. "If he doesn't, I will."

"Mel..."

She held up a hand. "Don't even. I'm going to get his info. You need to press charges."

"Melody Nikki. I will handle this."

"You did not just use both names."

"Do you want me to call Mom?"

"Jesus fuck, Eric. You could have been seriously injured because this asshole doesn't know when to stop drinking."

He glanced over at Libby, and despite the low light, she saw the concern in his face. She gave him a quick nod.

"Melody, I think Ana and I could stand to go home. Can you drive us?"

She looked like she wanted to argue, or maybe hit the drunk despite the presence of the cops, but she held herself together. "Fine. Let's go."

She started for the parking lot, with Ana close behind. Ana stopped in front of Zach for a moment, saying something Libby couldn't catch, and then ran after Melody.

Libby started to follow, but Eric caught her hand. He tugged her close, and she had to admit to herself that not all the feelings swirling inside of her were gratitude for his protection. He leaned in, and she felt his breath against his ear.

"Thanks. I owe you one."

"Later. I don't want my ride to leave without me."

"Lunch on Tuesday?"

She looked up and saw his gaze had darkened. "Uh, yeah. Sure. I need to go."

He squeezed her hand and let her go. She looked at him a moment more before heading for Melody's car with a detour to pick up her phone. It was in pieces, but she'd rather have the pieces in her possession rather than out for anyone to collect.

The ride back to Sunflower Falls was quiet. Libby didn't want to do anything to tip Melody's mood into something that couldn't be controlled.

When they parked at the motel, Melody let out a long breath. "Can you tell my mom that I'll talk to her tomorrow? I don't have the bandwidth tonight."

"Sure."

Libby headed into the office area and collected Mayzie and the puppies. Mrs. Keller petted Mayzie goodbye. "We went on a nice long walk together, so you don't have to worry about an evening stroll."

"Thanks, Mrs. Keller."

She stood up and looked Libby in the eye. "Something happened, didn't it?"

"I..."

Mrs. Keller held up her hand the same way Melody had earlier. "I'll get the story from my kids tomorrow. Take it easy tonight."

"Thank you."

Once she was back in the room and the puppies nestled in the bed she'd gotten for them, she called Greer from the motel phone. She'd have to get a new burner phone, as hers was toast. Mayzie climbed up on the bed and laid her head on Libby's thigh. Libby sighed and began petting Mayzie's head while she listened to the call ringing.

Eventually it went to Greer's voicemail. "Hey, Greer. Can you call me tomorrow when you get a chance? I'm okay. Just need some one-on-one time. I'm heading to bed, so don't bother calling back tonight."

She read off the number for the room and hung up. Mayzie climbed up closer and laid down next to her. Libby looked into the dog's eyes. "Thanks, Mayz."

It felt like she'd turned a corner tonight, but she didn't know which corner or what laid around it. She hated this feeling.

For now, she just had to focus on going to sleep. And then lunch on Tuesday.

eight

ERIC PULLED INTO HIS SPACE BEHIND THE OFFICE. HE'D ALREADY been on site this morning and back home for a shower. He and Melody had to get together to discuss project planning over the next six months as both Nora Sullivan and her wife were ready to hire them, as well as Caputo.

Melody had gone with him to sites yesterday, and while she'd come back fuming over something she'd refused to share, she said that he'd decided on a property that was going to require a complete tear down, but the land was perfect for what he wanted.

Libby was supposed to arrive in twenty minutes with the Mayzie and the puppies, and Melody would dog sit them while they were out.

When he walked in, he heard Melody talking to someone. He walked through the break area to the main office area and saw she was on her telephone. "Lose this number and don't ever call me again."

She slammed her phone down and he was glad that she'd gotten the heavy duty protective casing for when they were on site. Otherwise, it would probably be toast like Libby's had been Saturday night.

He winced again as he thought of the altercation. Even as he'd been trying to protect her from the drunk, his body couldn't stop cataloging the many ways it felt good to have her body against his.

When Melody looked up, glaring at him, he held up his hands. "Who was on the phone?"

"Dickhead Dad. I am sick of men trying to get into my life and tell me what to do."

"So..."

"Not you. We're business partners, even if you are my brother."

He sat down in his chair and rolled over next to her desk. "Besides Dad, does this have anything to do with Caputo?"

She looked up. "What did he say?"

Maybe he'd need to meet up with Zach to find out what the deal was with his new friend. "Absolutely nothing. I haven't seen him or Zach since Saturday. All you did yesterday when you came back from the site visits was growl at me. What happened?"

Melody leaned back in her chair and scrubbed her face. "Nothing. It's nothing. I can be perfectly professional. When's Libby coming in again?"

He checked his watch. He didn't like the change of topic, but when Melody didn't want to talk about something, even threatening to tear up posters of her favorite boy bands wouldn't get her to talk. "About fifteen minutes. Are you sure you can handle all the dogs?"

"Yeah. I need puppy time. Take as long as you need to for lunch." She lowered her hands. "I'm proud of you, big brother. Going out on a date."

"This isn't a date. Besides, she works for us."

"Technically, we can say she works for me as, if you told me to fire her, I'd tell you to go jump in the lake in the middle of January butt ass naked." Melody grinned at him. "And don't even try to go for the representation route as that's Greer. Libby's just a partner in the firm."

He shook his head and pushed back to go to his desk. "You're a bad influence."

"That's what little sisters are supposed to do. By the way, Greer left a message on my phone telling me to tell you to call her. She didn't say why."

He frowned. There hadn't seen a message from her in his voicemail. He opened his email program and searched for her address.

It popped up with a subject line to call her immediately. It had been in his spam folder. As he was going to open it, the front door opened and Libby walked in with Mayzie and the wagon trailing behind her. The email from Greer could wait. If it was really urgent, she had his phone number.

Melody got up and rushed around her desk. "You're early! Puppy time!"

Libby glanced first at Melody and then at Eric. "Uh-oh."

He shrugged. Saying anything at this point was inviting retribution from his sister. Libby dropped Mayzie's leash, and she came over to him. She did a quick sniff and licked his hand before heading over to the puppy containment area.

Melody crouched down, picked up Button, and cuddled the puppy against her face. Libby bit her lip and shifted on her feet. "Melody, do you need to talk?"

"Nope. I've got puppies, and you and my brother have a date. In fact, get out of here while you can." She stood up and made a shooing motion while keeping Button close. The puppy was wriggling and licking every inch of Melody's face that she could reach.

"I'll get Mayzie and the puppies settled first." Libby got

them sorted out and ten minutes later, they were on the front sidewalk.

He stood next to her as they watched Melody lock the front door and head back to the puppy area. She hadn't put Button down once.

Libby stood with her hands on her hips, staring at the door. "What just happened?"

"I have no clue. She was yelling at our dad on the phone when I came in the door, but wouldn't tell me what it was about. And she was in a bad mood after visiting potential homes with Caputo yesterday."

"She was with Tony?"

"Yeah, but I haven't talked with him or Zach, so I have no clue what happened."

She let out a long breath. "We should get going or she'll probably come out to yell at us."

He looked through the window and saw his sister sitting on the floor, covered with puppies. Mayzie was also in the containment area, but kept looking toward them. "Yeah."

They walked down to the diner only to find Mrs. Smith standing inside the door and every seat in the house taken. By kids, and some adults.

Mrs. Smith turned and smiled at them. "Apparently, the place hosting the eighth grade graduation luncheon had to cancel, and a parent called Nancy as backup. If you want, they're doing take out."

He looked down at Libby. "You okay with that?"

"Sure."

He thought of where he could take her. Melody obviously needed some personal time, and while he had planned what he wanted to talk with Libby about in public, it probably would be better with not everyone in the diner listening in.

They placed their order, and after a surprisingly brief wait, he led her back into the alley to head to his truck.

"Do you want to check in with Melody first?" Libby was watching where she stepped as she carried their drinks.

"No." He pulled his keys out of his pocket. "She made it very clear that she wasn't expecting us back for a bit. Once we get to where we're going, I'll text her to let her know we couldn't get a seat at the diner."

They got in range, and he unlocked the doors with his key fob. He followed Libby around to the passenger side and opened the door for her. Once she'd settled in, he ran around the bed of the truck and climbed in.

"You okay with eating outside?"

"Sure? Where are we going?"

He turned around in his seat to back out. "It's a little off the beaten path, but it's great on days like today."

Even better, they weren't likely to be interrupted by the random tourist, or even a local, out for a nature walk. As he headed to the little grove he'd found when he'd been a pissed-off teenager, they talked about the dogs. Libby had taken the puppies in to see Sam yesterday, and they'd passed their one-week check-up with flying colors. Even Button. Sam said that he didn't need to see them again for a few weeks unless Libby encountered any problems.

"Are you enjoying being a dog mom?"

She shrugged. "I'd never really considered it before. My dad refused to have pets of any kind, and when I got older, I was in class or studying all the time."

"What about after law school?"

"I was too busy working to get the business going with Greer. Contracts don't read themselves." She shot him a grin.

He laughed. Contracts would bore most people, but she seemed genuinely happy when she talked about her work.

"Did you ever get around to talking with Greer on Saturday?"

She shook her head. "I tried again on Sunday and yesterday, but no answer."

He frowned. "I had an email from her asking me to call her, but you walked in the door as I was about to read it."

"Did you?"

"No. She's got my number if it's something truly urgent."

She shifted in her seat to face him. "What about your uncle? Have you heard from him at all?"

"No. I told you, he doesn't contact anyone when he goes off on his vacation."

"Does he do this every year?"

"Yeah. He's been doing this for decades. I think from before I was born. I don't remember him not doing it, anyway."

She sighed. "I guess it's good I have the puppies, then."

"Don't forget Mayzie."

She laughed. "Mayzie won't let me forget Mayzie."

He shot a quick smile at her as he slowed to make the turn down the road that would take them to a hiking path that led to an overlook of the falls. "Are you sure you're not a dog mom? I don't think Mayzie will let you go."

She didn't answer him, and once he'd made the turn, he looked over to see her staring out the window. The angle of her shoulders made him think they carried the weight of the world.

Impulsively, he reached out and put his hand over hers where they were clenched together. "Hey, I'm sorry. What did I say?"

She shook her head.

"Just thinking about when I go back to the city."

Something in his chest pinched, and he rubbed at the

spot.

"I don't think I can take Mayzie with me. She probably wouldn't like the city. I need to move out of the apartment I was in, and I don't know what kind of place I can get."

"Why are you moving out?"

"I don't want anything my dad has a financial stake in."

"Did he lease it for you?"

She grimaced. "He owns it. I shouldn't have taken him up on the offer when I left law school, but he'd made it seem like a peace offering and graduation gift as we'd had an argument about what kind of law I wanted to practice."

"It wasn't?"

"Another thing I realized when I left. He was using the building staff to monitor my comings and goings and had access to the apartment."

It was his turn to grimace. "I'm sorry."

She laughed, but it had a caustic tone to it. "You know that poor little rich girl thing? It's really hard to feel bad for people who have all the privileges in the world, but for a lot of them, money just brings different problems." She quieted as he pulled over and parked. "Is this where we're eating?"

"Nope. We have to hike a little."

She brought up her foot again and grinned. He ignored the heat racing through his bloodstream. "Good thing I'm wearing my work site shoes."

"Good thing. If you can manage the drinks, I'll get the food and a blanket."

"Sure."

He grabbed the bag of food and pulled a work blanket from the storage tub in the bed of the truck. Then he led the way through the woods to the clearing he'd found all those years ago. He tried to ignore the little voice in the back of his mind asking why he was bringing her here when he hadn't brought anyone here, ever. Including Melody.

"Oh. This is gorgeous."

He grunted and set the bag down so he could spread the blanket out over the grass. They were in a pocket of the treeline close to the falls. Most of the tourists and locals stayed down below, which meant they wouldn't be seen. But they had a view of Sunflower Falls spread out below them and beyond that, Lake Ontario and the various little islands that dotted the coastline.

Even though it was early June, the namesake flowers for the falls and the town were beginning to grow along the creek which fed the falls.

"Who does this belong to?"

"Up here is private property. My uncle bought it before I was born. It's not well-marked, so most people don't bother coming up. Besides, the view that most people know is the falls themselves, and you can't see them from here."

Libby handed him his drink, and he sorted out the food. They ate in companionable silence for a while. Libby finally set down her container. "How did you find this place? Did your uncle tell you about it?"

He shook his head. "I'd had a fight with my dad and my uncle broke it up. Told me to get out of the house and cool down."

"You fought with your dad?"

"Yeah. He's...not the best. I think I told you that before?"

"Yes. I'm sorry."

He shrugged one shoulder. "It is what it is."

She reached over and squeezed his knee. After a moment, he shifted, and she pulled her hand away. He immediately regretted the loss of the contact. "Thanks." Even he could hear the growl in the single word.

"Just because something is a certain way doesn't mean it doesn't suck."

He drew in a breath and let it out slowly. He wasn't sure

why, but having her here, listening to him, truly listening to him and not telling him to let it go already, made it easier to talk.

"I don't know what it is with my dad. He had every advantage. Hell, he had Stef just a year older than him. My grandparents gave him every opportunity, but he prefers to run cons as often as he can get away with them. My mom finally kicked him out, but he'd always come back. Until that time. I came home early from school and found him yelling at her in the kitchen. Mom had been on the phone with Uncle Stef when he arrived, but I didn't know that. I just knew he was threatening my mom, and I attacked."

"How old were you?"

Eric drew up his knees and rested his arms around them. He kept his sight on a sailboat heading out from the nearby harbor to the deeper part of the lake. "Seventeen. Old enough to know better, but young enough to not listen to any kind of reason."

"Did he fight back?"

"Yeah, but he didn't get many blows in. He was drunk. I wasn't. Then, Uncle Stef was there." He thought back to that day, and the emotions he'd felt then flooded back. If his dad was in front of him now, he'd do the same thing again. The man had never once apologized for what he'd done to them over the years.

He heard Libby clear her throat and glanced over at her. The light wind blew her hair into her face, and she tried to hook it behind her ear, but it wouldn't stay. He reached over and did the same, letting his fingers linger against the soft skin behind her ear. She leaned into his touch, and he leaned over.

Kissed her.

He hadn't meant to, but her lips felt so good and tasted of Nancy's famous chicken salad sandwich. When she didn't immediately respond, he pulled back, but before he got far, she reached up and gripped his head.

She pressed against him, her lips molding to his. She gasped, and he shifted his kisses from her mouth down to her neck. He felt her fumbling with her other hand, and then she pressed it against his head, her fingers tangling in his hair.

He nipped a particularly sweet spot on her neck. She moaned. "Eric."

"What?" It wasn't louder than a mumble, but he didn't want to leave this slice of heaven.

"Come here." She tugged on his hair when he didn't immediately move.

Reluctantly, he pressed another kiss against her neck and lifted his head. "Yeah?"

She lifted her head and pressed her lips against his. This time, he let her lead. When he needed closer contact, he shifted and pressed a leg against hers. She shifted and made space for him between her legs.

Soon, they were both breathing heavily. They mutually broke the kiss and stared at each other.

He was the first to blink. "Time out?"

She continued panting a little and nodded. "Maybe not in public?"

"No one should be able to see us, but yeah."

At that moment, as if the universe took his statement as a challenge, a drone rose above the falls.

He rolled away from her and pushed up from the ground. Since he didn't know who was controlling the drone, and didn't want to piss off some parent if it was a kid, he went for a short walk back to the tree line. He rubbed the back of his neck and tried to get a grip on his emotions.

Making out with Libby Hartwell had not in any way

been on his to do list for the day. He'd only intended to share a friendly lunch with her. Even coming out here, that had been the extent of his plans.

He glared at the nearby maple. It was tempting to bash his head against it to knock some sense back into his brain.

"Eric?"

"Coming." Lunch. They were having lunch. A nice, friendly lunch. Out in public, even if nobody was in sight. He began walking back and saw the drone was still circling.

He didn't want to pay the replacement cost for it, and so resisted finding a rock to throw at it. With his luck, it would belong to some little kid, and he'd make the kid cry. Not how he wanted to spend the rest of his day.

He sat down on the blanket and picked his sandwich back up. Thankfully, Nancy and Bob served homemade chips with their sandwiches, so he didn't have to worry about cold fries. Besides the uncomfortable feeling of frustrated desire, cold fries were one of life's worst experiences.

Libby brushed her hands free of crumbs as she finished her sandwich. She took a sip of her drink and then set it down on the ground next to her.

"Just to remind you, you're not the only person with a shit dad."

He sighed. "Yeah, I know."

She was silent for a bit and then turned to him. "Good."

They finished their meal, and with little talking, they began gathering everything up. Libby put the trash in the bag, and Eric gathered up the blanket. As they began walking back to the truck, Libby reached out and took his hand.

"Thank you for showing me this." She paused for a few steps, and he ducked under a branch. When she cleared it, she squeezed his hand. "Thank you for everything. Everything."

nine

LIBBY TRIED TO SETTLE THE PUPPIES DOWN FOR THEIR LATE afternoon nap. It didn't help that they were still wound up from playing with Melody. Only Mayzie seemed at all inclined for a nap, and she'd bundled herself up in a blanket on the bed as soon as they walked in the door and Libby removed her harness.

Trying to get them settled was a welcome distraction from her thoughts, which wanted to dissect in detail exactly what she'd done with Eric up at the top of the falls. That kiss had been more than a kiss, and a hell of a lot hotter than she had ever gotten with her former fiancè.

Whose name she was conveniently forgetting.

Herman.

Her ex-fiancè's name was Herman.

She was a mess. She spent months engaged to a man, and a week after she left him, completely forgot his name, all because of the kiss of a man she barely knew. A very hot man with matching lips, but that was no excuse. Right?

Just as she was finally getting them quieted down, someone knocked on the door. The puppies immediately began yipping in excitement and tried jumping up over the barrier of the crate she kept them in. Two of them made it over and she realized they'd grown so much in the last week that she already needed something with bigger walls.

She picked up the two escape artists and left the others in the crate, trying to climb the walls. Since so few people had knocked on her door in her time in Sunflower Falls, she assumed it was most likely Mrs. Keller. Shock filled her when she checked the peephole and found someone on the other side who was decidedly not Mrs. Keller.

Libby unlocked and opened the door as fast as she could with one arm filled with writhing puppies desperate to be free. "Greer. What are you doing here?"

Greer waved. "Oh, puppies!" She reached out and plucked one from Libby's arm.

The help was welcome, but she still couldn't believe her friend and business partner was standing at her door.

"What are you doing here?" Especially when she was probably most in need of her friend.

Greer winced. "Not in public."

Libby realized she was blocking the door and stepped back to make room for her. "Sorry. I'm a bit distracted." And little of the distraction had to do with all the dogs.

Greer rubbed the head of the puppy in her hands. Luckily, not Button or Melody would be having a fit. "I can see."

After Greer sat down on the foot of the bed—Mayzie only briefly looked up from her nap before snuggling back down into the blanket—Libby set the puppy she still held back in the crate.

"Do you want something to drink? I can offer you bottled water or some alcoholic seltzer."

"I'm good. Thanks. You should probably sit down."

Libby recognized the tone in her business partner's voice. It rarely meant good news for them. Deciding *she* could use the alcoholic seltzer, she went to the mini-fridge and pulled one out. She sat down by the head of the bed and popped the top. "What?"

"Your dad's filed for guardianship over you."

Libby almost dropped the can, but caught it at the last moment. "He did what?"

"He filed to place you under guardianship."

Libby watched Greer's face, but knew deep down in her gut that this was not a joke. Her father truly had filed to have her rights taken away. "How do you know this?"

"Because I was watching for it. I knew as soon as you left he'd pull something. Wasn't expecting this, but I'm not surprised. I've already contacted Phaedra, and she's got her dad ready for your call."

Phaedra Billings had been her somewhat nemesis in law school. Their fathers had been at odds with each other for decades. Libby just bet that Mr. Billings was rubbing his hands together over the possibility of going head-to-head with her father.

Libby rubbed her face. This news certainly put her kiss with Eric in perspective. "Do I have to head back to the city now?"

"I doubt it, but I'm sure Mr. Billings will give you the full rundown."

She flopped back on the bed, and Mayzie lifted her head enough to nuzzle her cheek. "What the hell is his deal, Greer?"

"Maybe you'll be able to find out with all this."

Libby's laugh was filled with lemon juice. "That's a great way to find out why your father hates you. Have him file for guardianship and go to court over it."

Greer reached over and squeezed her leg. "Here. Call Mr. Billings on my phone. I've got his number programmed. And I put him on retainer for B&H in case your dad wants to drag the business into this, too."

Libby took the phone Greer held out and saw her friend had already unlocked it and opened the contact page.

She spent the next hour talking with Mr. Billings and retaining him as her counsel. She could stay in Sunflower Falls for the time being as he would act as her agent in court, especially as he had her phone number and could easily reach her.

When she hung up, she blew out a breath. "This sucks, Greer."

"Yeah. By the way, your dad is not the only trouble dad we need to deal with."

Libby pushed up. "Your dad is a saint."

Greer laughed. "Yes, he is. And, no, not my dad. Eric and Melody's dad."

"What?" Libby felt a moment of déjà vu thanks to her earlier conversation with Eric.

"Eric and Melody's dad is going around, contacting people about the real story behind them and their relationship with their uncle. He's saying he's willing to sell the story to the highest bidder." Greer made big air quotes around the real.

"What story? That their uncle stepped in and was a better father figure to them than their dad could ever be? Melody's told me a couple stories, and Eric mentioned something today about getting into a fight with him when he was drunk. Eric was only a teenager at the time."

Greer's lip curled up. "Seriously? He sounds like a bigger asshole than I assumed, and I was already assuming a lot."

Libby got up off the bed. "Come on. I'm hungry, and Mayzie needs to go for a walk. How long are you staying?"

"Mind if I stay here overnight? I don't particularly want to drive back tonight."

Libby paused in getting Mayzie's harness onto her. "How did you get up here? I've got your car."

"And you're keeping it. I borrowed one of my cousin's cars. I got a feeling your dad's got someone watching me, and I didn't want a record of anything."

Libby went over and hugged Greer. "Thank you. I don't know what I did to deserve you."

"You helped me study for L1 Contracts. I never would have passed that course without you. I owe you my entire career."

Libby laughed. "Come on. I think it will be easier if we can leave the puppies here, but let me call Mrs. Keller."

"Keller? Any relation to Eric and Melody?"

"Their mom." Libby called down to the front office, and Mrs. Keller agreed to take the puppies while they were out walking around town.

They dropped the puppies off in the office, and Libby introduced Greer to Mrs. Keller. They liked each other instantly, and Libby almost had to pull Greer out the door. "Dinner is calling."

They walked the couple blocks to the downtown area with Mayzie periodically stopping to sniff the grass and other interesting spots along the way. A couple cars honked as they passed, and Libby waved when she recognized the people in them.

Greer looked at her. "Since when did you make friends with random strangers?"

"What do you mean? I know those people."

"How long have you been here?"

She stopped next to Mayzie, who'd found a very interesting piece of lamp post. "You know exactly how long I've been here."

"And I have never seen you wave to people honking at you."

Libby rolled her eyes. "We live in New York City, Greer. Of course I'm not going to wave at someone honking at me.

They're likely cursing me out for some unknown reason. This is Sunflower Falls. They were just saying hi with the double tap."

Greer shook her head. "I am definitely not staying any longer than I need to. I do not need to be waving at anyone honking at me whether they're saying a friendly hi or fuck you."

They moved on, and on the next block, she saw Sam coming out of the diner. He spotted them and waved.

Libby and Greer waited for a couple of cars to turn and then crossed the street. Sam continued waiting outside the diner. When they got close, he squatted down and held his hand out to Mayzie. "How are you doing? Is your mom giving you all the loving?"

Libby glanced over at Greer, expecting her friend to be ready with an eye roll. Instead, Greer was watching Sam with her brows raised.

Mayzie leaned against Libby, but consented for Sam to scratch her neck just behind an ear. "She's doing good."

"Excellent. It was good to see the puppies yesterday. Any changes since then?"

"Nope. They're with Mrs. Keller right now."

He smiled and stood up. "Great. Hi, I'm Sam Rivers, town vet." He held out his hand to Greer.

Greer smiled. "Greer Branford. City girl. Do you always greet the pets first?"

"Always. If the pet accepts you, you're in good company. Planning on staying long?"

"No. I'm headed back tomorrow."

"I hope you'll consider coming back some time. We've got great sailing and other outdoor activities."

"I'm sure you do."

Libby noticed that neither of them seemed to be in a hurry to release the other's hand. When they didn't continue the conversation, but stood there smiling at each other, she cleared her throat.

They continued to ignore her. She cleared her throat louder. That seemed to break through to Greer, who broke the handshake.

"We should probably go eat."

"Yeah. Nice to meet you, Greer Branford."

"You, too, Sam Rivers."

Libby waited until Sam had walked down the block and opened his truck door. She leaned into Greer. "I hear there's a nearby pharmacy if you need to go buy condoms."

"Shut up."

Libby laughed. "Come on, we should get our order in now."

They headed inside and gave their take out order to Ana. "It'll be about twenty minutes. Do you want to wait?"

Libby looked at the filled diner and shook her head. "We'll be back. Mayzie could use a longer walk."

They headed out and continued walking down the block. As they passed Secrets and Whimsies, she glanced inside and saw Mrs. Smith at the register. She looked up and waved at them, gesturing for them to come in.

"What's this?"

"You'll love it. Mrs. Smith has everything."

"Mrs. Smith? What is she? A retired spy?"

Libby laughed. "No. But she seems to know everything about this town." Libby wondered what Mrs. Smith might know about Eric and Melody's dad.

Once inside, Libby introduced Greer to Mrs. Smith. The older woman held out her hand to Greer. "Nice to meet you. Are you enjoying our little town so far?"

Greer smiled and shook her hand. "It's nice. I haven't seen much of the town besides driving in. But it seems to be treating Libby well, which is all I ask."

Mrs. Smith grinned. "Libby, and Mayzie," she added when Mayzie woofed, "have been a wonderful addition to Sunflower Falls. Would you like a cup of tea?"

Libby shook her head. "We just ordered take out from the diner and I'm showing Greer around while they get it ready."

"Excellent." She bent down and reached under the counter for something. When she came up, she handed each of them a small packet. "These are samples I received in the mail this morning. Have it for your dessert, and let me know what you think."

They thanked her and assured her Libby would get back to her with their thoughts. They headed back out onto the street, and Libby pointed out Eric and Melody's storefront.

Greer cupped her hands around her face and looked inside. "Think we can get them to do some filming in here? It's bare bones, but the architectural details are fabulous."

"Talk to Eric. You're the one who handles this kind of thing."

"Speaking of Eric..." Greer looked back over her shoulder and waggled his brows. "What's going on between you two?"

Libby looked around, but everyone who was downtown tonight seemed to be on a mission. Most were heading in and out of the diner. "Not in public."

"Fine. But you know he never got back to me."

"Not my problem. He told me he saw an email from you, but hadn't had a chance to open it. And, if it was urgent, you had his phone number."

Greer let out a sigh. "He was right. If it was truly urgent, I could have called. He'll just have to be surprised by me showing up in person."

Libby paused as Mayzie took her time sniffing out a flower box in front of the next storefront. "Text him or something to warn him. He might be planning on being on-site tomorrow morning."

Greer pulled her phone out. "You're right. Hey, do you want to head back? The food should be ready soon."

"In a moment. I want to show you something."

"What?"

"Just come on."

Libby led the way down to one of the paths that led to the public access beach. Greer started complaining about the sand lining the path getting into her shoes, but Libby ignored her. Mayzie started pulling on her leash as she realized where they were going.

They turned a corner in the path and the beach and Lake Ontario with the barrier islands spread out in front of them. The sun was getting low in the sky, highlighting the tree lines of some of the islands.

"Whoa."

"Isn't it gorgeous?"

"Yeah. A lot different from going out to the Hamptons."

"I think I want to buy a house here, Greer."

Libby felt her friend's sharp gaze turn to her. She kept her focus on the view. If Greer pressed her on why, she wouldn't be able to explain other than it was so different from what she'd known. This view alone would be worth it, but she'd also fallen in love with Sunflower Falls.

She'd never believed that she could fall in love in a week.

It was fun to go into the diner and see what Nancy had put up for the daily special. Walking Mayzie around had exposed her to so many people who were just friendly. She felt like she could actually find a place for herself and make friends who didn't have preconceived ideas of what she must be like.

Greer placed an arm around her shoulders. "Permanently, or a summer place?"

Libby shrugged, but not enough to dislodge Greer's embrace. "Maybe a summer place to start? But if my father is determined to pursue this guardianship thing, I'll probably just have to rent."

"What about renting here for this summer, and I go clean out your place of your stuff? I can check with Mr. Billings about what I'd need to get everything, and we'll make a clean break for you."

As she thought about it, Libby realized the path ahead of her was clear. She didn't know what it would be like to run the business without Greer close by, but technology was a lovely thing. She could easily review contracts, and do the back end of the business from home with a good internet connection.

"That sounds good." She let out a long breath. "Thank you."

Greer squeezed her. "I'm glad to see you finally stepping away from your dad. I know you wanted more, but he's got issues."

"Yeah. I wonder what my mom ever saw in him."

"Are you okay with never knowing?"

Libby slipped her shoes off and let her feet sink into the sun-warmed sand. "I'll have to be, won't I? I'm hoping to get some answers from Eric and Melody's uncle, but they'll still be his impressions and memories. I can't ever ask her directly."

Greer also slipped her shoes off and they began walking down the beach toward the more public part. There were still a few families hanging out, but most everyone seemed to be packing up for the day.

Greer bumped her shoulder against Libby's. "What's going on between you and Eric?"

"Nothing."

Greer hummed, but didn't challenge her further. "I'm just saying that if you move up here for the summer, not only would you get away from your dad, but you'll also have some time to see what he's like. Take things easy."

"What is it with you and matchmaking? Don't you remember the wedding I ran away from a little over a week ago?"

Libby didn't realize that Greer had stopped until she was a few feet away. She turned back and saw that Greer had thrown her head back. She walked back to where her friend stood. Mayzie whined a bit and nudged one of Greer's fists.

"Greer?"

"I'm sorry."

"What?" Confused, Libby took Greer's other hand in hers and squeezed. "Whatever it is, it's okay."

Greer shook her head. "I should have told you sooner."

"Just say it. I'm imagining a lot of not great stuff right now." She didn't think Greer would ever betray her, but why would her friend be keeping secrets from her?

"Herman actually ran off with his secretary. Everyone thinks you're a jilted bride, and that you're in hiding because you're embarrassed. They also think your dad had no clue about either of you, and is the most wounded person in all of this, since he paid for everything."

Libby blinked. Tried to parse out exactly what Greer said. Her brain finally latched onto the most important part. "Everyone thinks I'm a jilted bride?"

Greer nodded. "I was trying to figure out what I was going to say and who to tell the news to when Herman's best man called me trying to get in touch with you. He wanted to let you know Herman called him from the airport. They left that morning."

Libby sank down onto the sand. Mayzie began licking her face, and she realized she was crying.

"I'm okay, Mayzie. Sit. Sit." She pushed down on Mayzie's hindquarters until the dog sat, her tail flinging sand in all directions. "Did he tell anyone else?"

"Apparently, he left a letter for his mom, and she refused to give it to your dad. She's also initiated divorce proceedings against her husband."

"Good for her." Libby rubbed her face and then began laughing. Mayzie cocked her head, but Libby couldn't stop.

After a few minutes that left her abs feeling like she'd done a ridiculous amount of planks, she pushed up.

"Come on, Greer. Let's go get dinner. I need to celebrate." Wherever they were, she wished Herman and his secretary the best of luck. Both of them were going to need new jobs.

And when she and Greer were done with dinner, she was going house hunting.

ten

ERIC LOOKED OUT OVER LAKE ONTARIO AS HE SIPPED HIS COFFEE. The view from what would be Caputo's back deck was killer. If he ever sold, he'd get top dollar for this alone. In fact, most of what Caputo was paying for this property was for the view. He glanced over at his coffee supplier for the morning. "You're sure?"

"Yes. I can send him a cease and desist letter that is extremely threatening. Since he contacted me by email and I don't have any other way to contact him, it'll have to be sent that way. You don't have an address for him, do you?" Greer sipped from her own to-go cup.

"No. And before you ask, I'm pretty sure that Melody doesn't have an address for him, either. He's never really stayed in one place long enough for us to send him things. Not that we want to. Mom had a hell of a time serving him with the divorce paperwork."

"I'm sorry."

He laughed. "I'm not. She should have dumped his ass long before she finally did. Send the letter. Make it as threatening as you can. Did he demand money?"

She shook her head. "I'm sure it's in his plan to do that,

though. I can and will shut this down for you. You're at least easy."

"Dealing with my dad is never easy."

"Well, easier than dealing with Libby's dad, then."

His attention pricked up at that, but he tried to be smooth and waited until he'd taken another sip of coffee before asking the natural question. "What's going on with Libby's dad?"

Greer let out a sigh as she walked around the backyard of the property. "Normally, I'd let Libby share because this is her story, but I need you to watch out for her while she's up here, and I'm not sure she'd share with you in a timely manner. Her father filed for guardianship."

He frowned as he racked his brain to figure out what she was saying. "I don't understand. What's guardianship? Like a kid gets a guardian when their parents die or can't care for them?"

"Kind of. Basically, someone, either another person or a corporate entity, files with the court saying that a person is incapable of caring for themselves either personally, financially, or both. If the court agrees with the evidence, the person placed in guardianship is declared legally incapacitated. Her father wants to take all of her rights away."

Holy shit. He thought his dad was a complete fucker. "Can she fight this?"

"Yes, and she is. We've hired an attorney who specializes in this and happens to also hate her dad. But if her father finds out where she is, we don't want him taking her away from here."

"Damn." He wasn't sure what to say to that. He took a few more sips of coffee, hoping the caffeine would help make the necessary connections in his brain. "Does she need to go deeper into hiding?"

"We don't think so, but I can call you if something changes."

"Do that. We'll keep an eye on her."

Greer walked back to him and looked him dead in the eye. He held the contact until she finally nodded. "I appreciate that. She's my business partner, but she's also my best friend. She doesn't deserve the shit hand life's dealt her, and I'm determined to help her make a better life for herself."

"What about her fiancè? Will he be coming around at all?"

Greer laughed. "Nope. He's off in the islands somewhere with his secretary."

"What? He took off for the planned honeymoon when he found out she'd left?"

"No. I'll give him that. He's not a complete asshole. Just no spine when it comes to Libby's dad. He ran off with his secretary the morning of the wedding. Turns out his escape was discovered first, so everyone thinks Libby's a jilted bride with her feelings hurt. Obviously, not the case."

Eric cleared his throat as he realized what Greer was sharing with him. "Obviously. So, he's out of the picture?"

"Completely." She lifted her coffee in salute to him. "He was barely in the picture to begin with, but Libby had this unfortunate habit of trying to make her dad happy. I'm still surprised she held her line when he wanted her to join the family practice. Until the wedding, setting up shop with me was her only real moment of rebellion."

"Why are you telling me all this?"

"Because I think you're a decent guy, Eric. Even if you give sandpaper with a grit of 24 a run for its money."

He almost choked on the sip of coffee he'd just taken. Greer had better be thankful he didn't spray her with it.

Once he'd cleared his throat, he laughed. "You've been waiting to use that line, haven't you?"

"Yup. I did my research while I was wooing you and Melody."

"If you think I'm that rough, why did you want us as clients?"

"Because you know your shit and you look good on camera. I can get you deals and make myself, and Libby, a lot of money while we're doing it. Speaking of, have you lined up your next project yet?"

"No. But you're looking at one of the possibilities. I still need to talk with the owner. He'd also look good on camera, but he does not know his shit."

Greer looked at the house and wrinkled her nose. "How in the hell are you going to renovate this?"

"We're not. We're going to tear it down and start over. Our client has plans, and if we can get him to agree to letting us film, even if he doesn't want to be on camera, I think we'll have the opportunity to work with some real class brands."

Greer tapped her fingernail on her teeth. "Which brands?"

They talked shop for the next twenty minutes before Greer had to head out. "Put me in touch with the client if you need to. I can sweet talk almost anyone into doing what I want them to do."

"That's a dangerous superpower."

She winked. "I know it. Libby helps keep me in check. I'll call you when I have more information on the guardianship."

"Thanks."

He watched her head out around the house and was glad she didn't trip on any of the broken paving. They were going to have to do a complete haul out of everything on site first. Caputo was supposed to close on the property in a couple weeks, and then they could get started. That should be enough time for them to convince him that filming the renovation would help add to the rental value in the future.

Eric finished up with taking the photos of the site that he needed and headed back into town. Melody was at the Sullivan site today, and it was one of Libby's days off from the office. It couldn't hurt to check in with her. Make sure she had what she needed. Especially with the puppies.

But when he went to the motel, her car wasn't in the lot. He didn't want to bother his mom or tip her off about anything, so he headed to the office. There, he found Libby's car parked in back.

Frowning, he stared at her car for a few minutes before parking next to it. Usually, Libby would walk from the motel when she was working in the office. It was easier with the puppies. And she said that walking over also helped her save on gas.

The back door was locked when he tried it, so he pulled out his keys and headed in. Libby was sitting in the dark in his chair, spinning around in it.

He flipped the lights for the office area on. She yelped and spun to face him.

"You okay?"

Her eyes were wide, but she nodded.

"Want a bottle of water?"

She shook her head.

Libby was normally a lot more talkative, and neither the puppies nor Mayzie were present. "What's going on, Libby?"

She took a deep breath, and he did his best to ignore what it did for her breasts. When she let it out, she closed her eyes. "Sorry. I wasn't expecting you for a while. And I didn't want anyone thinking someone was in here when I wasn't actually supposed to be working."

"Okay. But that doesn't really answer my question. Did something happen?"

She shook her head, then nodded, then shook it again. Then she rubbed her face. "Sorry, I've got a lot on my mind."

Not sure what to do after the information that Greer had revealed to him, he went over and pulled Libby into his embrace. He took his time so she knew she could pull away any time she needed to, but instead she damn near launched herself the remaining distance, wrapping her arms around him in a tight hug.

"Libby?"

"Just let me enjoy this."

He laughed. "Okay."

According to his mental clock, they stood there in silence for a couple of minutes. He brushed a light kiss on the side of her head. So light he barely disturbed her hair that she'd pulled up into one of those messy buns. She rubbed her face against his chest.

After another couple of minutes, he squeezed her. "Libby?"

She let out a breath and then patted one of his pecs. He resisted the urge to flex. "Thanks. I'm guessing Greer probably told you everything."

He thought for a second about lying, but he never wanted to lie to her. "Yeah. Your dad's a fucking asshole, and your fiancè jilted you."

Libby wiped her cheeks, and he realized she'd started crying. He reached up and ran his thumb under one eye. "Damn, baby, don't do that."

"Baby?"

"Just run with it. Neither of them are worth it."

"Oh, I know. It's just a lot to process. Anyway. The reason I'm here is because I want to rent a house here."

He blinked. He had not been expecting that. "Rent? Where?"

"Somewhere on the lake. Preferably fenced so the dogs can run around as they get bigger, but with my dad doing what he's doing, I may as well stay here for at least the summer."

He really had not been expecting that. "Did you just decide this?"

"No. Well, I decided last night. I talked it over with Greer, and she agreed it was a good idea."

Considering everything else Greer had told him about earlier, she could have at least thrown this in there. "Okay, but most everything's probably rented, at least for the summer. At least what's close in to town. I don't want you being out in the middle of nowhere."

"It's not your decision, is it?"

She was right, but he didn't have to like it. "At least let me introduce you to Mrs. Troy."

"She's the real estate agent, right?"

"Yeah. She'll know which properties are available, and which aren't." And hopefully, she'd have something that wasn't completely out of town and closer to help if Libby needed it.

He called up Mrs. Troy, and she assured him she could see Libby right away. Once he hung up, he dug out his keys. "Come on."

"What? I can drive myself."

"You can drive yourself, but I'd rather you didn't." Not after what Greer had shared.

She gave him the evil eye, but decided it must not have been worth the fight. Libby got up and grabbed her purse from the back of the chair.

The Troys lived close to where Eric and Melody had grown up, and where his uncle still lived. He was pretty sure Mr. Troy was determined to be planted in the backyard with his prize roses when he passed.

Over the years, Mrs. Troy had converted the front two rooms of the house into a small office for her real estate business. When he parked on the street a couple houses down, he saw the front door stood open, and she had put up some fancy signage in front. A young couple was walking out the door with a couple of kids racing around them.

He and Libby walked over, and one of the men started getting the two kids settled into a van. The other guy looked over at them with a grin. "If you're house hunting here, Evelyn Troy's the best. She just got us hooked up with our first house."

Eric smiled at them. "Congratulations. Welcome to Sunflower Falls."

The man grinned back at him and held out a hand. "You're local? Nice to meet you. Hopefully, we'll see you around town."

He shook the offered hand. "It's hard to miss people around here. Have a great day."

Eric put his hand on the small of Libby's back and steered her to the house. While he was happy for the young family, they didn't have a lot of time for chitchat.

Mrs. Troy was standing at the door, and waved at them. "Come on in. I've got about fifteen minutes before another appointment."

She waved at the family, and then stepped in behind them and closed the door. "Sorry. It's been busy today between showings, closings, and getting ready for the Street Fest."

Eric gestured to Libby. "This is Libby Hartwell, she's

interested in a rental for the summer. Closer to town would be good."

Libby glared at him. "I can speak for myself. And closer to town isn't a huge priority for me."

Mrs. Troy laughed. "I'm glad to hear it. We have a couple of properties left that are close to town, but pretty much everything is at least partially booked. If you're thinking of renting again for next summer, I can guarantee you'll have a wider selection if you want to book now."

Libby shook her head. "Just this summer right now. Also, I'm fostering a mom dog and her litter of five puppies, so it has to be pet-friendly, and preferably have a fenced-in yard."

Mrs. Troy walked over to where she had a sleek desk and computer setup. "Have a seat. We can go over the possibilities."

Libby sat down, but Eric stayed where he was standing.

Mrs. Troy looked over at him, and she saw one of her eyebrows lift. "Eric?"

"I'll just look around and see what's up for sale." One wall of the office area had been set up to display her listings. For the most part, Eric knew which properties were going up for sale ahead of time, but there were always some that got past him. As he studied the listings, he kept an ear out for which properties Mrs. Troy was highlighting for Libby.

Most of them were on the outskirts of town but with lake access. He knew Libby would probably like that as he'd seen her walking the access path to the beach with Mayzie several times.

"Now, this one might actually best fit your needs. I just got a call this morning from the owner, who had to cancel their short-term rentals for the summer. There's an issue with one of the bathrooms and the adjoining space in the finished basement that's going to require some renovations over the summer, but if you're willing to live in a construction zone, I'm sure I can get you a deal for it."

Eric looked over. "Which property is this?"

Mrs. Troy smiled. "You remember Andy Kavanaugh?"

"Yeah. He was a year behind me in Melody's class."

"He bought the big house over on Jones Road last year. He'd been planning on doing some updates, but the family that rented the house last week reported a water leak, and he found that whoever had finished the basement had done a horrible job with the plumbing."

Eric winced. He could only imagine what was going on there. Until he and Melody had set up shop, most of the renovation crews came from outside Sunflower Falls. "It's just the basement, though?"

"So far." She turned to Libby. "It's not on the lakefront, but it's close by and it's usually rented out to large families. I can guarantee there's enough space for you and the dogs that the basement renovations shouldn't cause any issues."

And, depending on who Andy hired, there would be people around Libby and the house on a regular basis. The house was on the other side of town from the motel, but it wasn't far from his place, or Melody's.

"Does it have a fenced-in yard?"

Mrs. Troy shook her head. "I don't think so. We don't have many fenced-in yards for the rentals."

Eric went over and sat down next to Libby. "Take a look at it. If you like it, I can talk with Andy. Provided he's willing, I can build a temporary run for you."

"Okay. Can we see it today?"

Mrs. Troy grinned at them. "Let me call him."

Twenty minutes later, they were pulling up to the house on Jones Road. Andy Kavanaugh was standing in front, his lab on a leash next to him. He held out a hand to Eric. "Hey, man. How are you doing?"

"Good. I hear you're having plumbing issues."

Andy laughed, which was a good sign. He'd gotten out of the Navy about five years ago and had jumped from job to job. His latest venture was acquiring rental properties. "Just a few." He looked over at Libby. "You're the one looking to rent?"

"I am."

He looked between them, but didn't say anything further. "Come on in. I can show you the areas that I don't expect to be impacted by the renovation. Mrs. Troy also said you've got a dog?"

"A dog and five puppies. I'm fostering them until they're able to be adopted out."

He smiled as he unlocked the front door. "Sam roped you in?"

She smiled back, and Eric had to force himself to not growl at Andy. For one, his dog would growl right on back. "She's going to need fencing for the dogs. Would that be an issue?"

Andy must have sensed something because he looked at him over Libby's head and raised both of his eyebrows. "I don't currently have any fencing here, but if you want to build something, go ahead. I'd want to approve the design, though."

"Of course."

Andy quickly turned back to the door and opened it. Eric had the distinct impression he was doing his best to hide a smile. The tour of the house took all of fifteen minutes since they weren't going through the basement. There was a separate entrance that the renovation crew was going to use, and they were scheduled to start the next week.

"How soon can I move in?"

Andy glanced at Eric again, but he just held up his hands and shook his head. He turned his attention back to Libby. "How about we get the fencing installed first? Eric, how long will that take you?"

He thought over his schedule with the Sullivan house and what he needed to do to prep for the work on Caputo's. "Probably a couple of days. If it's okay with you, I can probably do it over this weekend." It would wipe out his weekend, but it would be worth it.

Andy nodded. "I'm supposed to go watch Alex play, so shoot me the plans."

"That's right. They're in the championships."

"Yeah, the whole family's flying out tomorrow night. Don't tell anyone, but he's planning on retiring when this season's over."

"Lips are sealed. Good luck to him."

"Thanks. I'll let him know."

Andy and Libby finalized a few details, and he said he'd have Mrs. Troy send her the rental agreement.

When they were done, they climbed into his truck, and Libby let out a long breath. He glanced at her before putting the truck into gear. "You okay?"

She grinned at him, and it was so bright, he was glad he was wearing his sunglasses. "I've got my own place. For the first time ever, I have a place of my own that my father had absolutely no role in."

He smiled back. "Congratulations." He absolutely would have the fencing finished by the end of the weekend, even if he had to pull his crew in on overtime. Knowing Libby would be in Sunflower Falls for the entire summer had his thoughts churning in directions he probably should shut down. But he couldn't quite convince himself that he should turn off the warm glow.

eleven

"AND THE FIRST PLACE WINNER OF THE ELEVENTH ANNUAL START of Summer Street Fair Pet Show is Mayzie Hartwell!"

Libby glanced down at Mayzie, who seemed to take her win in stride as people rushed up to them and congratulated her while petting Mayzie. The emcee came over and pinned a huge blue ribbon thing onto Mayzie's harness. The field of contestants hadn't been deep, and from what Libby gathered, most of them had already won in previous years.

After the ceremony was over, Melody and Ana came over with the puppies. They had grown so much in the last couple of weeks that the netting that had kept them in the wagon was no longer enough. They each had individual harnesses with short leashes which were attached to the inner frame of the wagon. Luckily, they were pretty well behaved out in public.

Mayzie did a quick count of the puppies and gave them each a lick. They tumbled over each other to touch noses with her. It was ridiculously cute, and Libby hoped that having them out in public like this would help generate some interest in adopting them when they were ready.

Melody unhooked Button from the wagon frame and picked her up. "Want to go see the dunking booth? Eric's the current victim."

"What?" She and Eric had talked about meeting up later in the day, but all he'd said when she told him Mrs. Smith had signed Mayzie up for the dog show was he'd have to miss it because of a prior commitment.

Melody's grin was downright evil. "The Sunflower Falls Business Association is the sponsor of the dunking booth, and members are expected to sign up for at least a one-hour time slot. I did it last year, so it's Eric's turn this year."

Ana smiled as she began pulling the wagon. "They also have a side bet going. If Eric gets dunked more times than Melody did, then he has to not only buy the crew's drinks for the annual Ice Party, but also for the summer cookout."

Libby glanced over at Melody, who was nuzzling Button. "How many times were you dunked last year?"

"Ten."

"Is that a lot?"

"Probably average. Come on. I don't want to miss the chance of putting him over and winning."

When they were at the dunking booth, Eric was sitting on a wooden plank, wearing swim trunks and a t-shirt—and soaked to the skin. The t-shirt was molded to the muscles of his chest, and Libby hoped no one saw her lick her lips.

Zach and Tony were standing off to the side, shit-talking to him. But they immediately stopped when a Black adult stepped up with a kid who looked like they were around nine or ten.

Eric cheered from the tank. "Hey Cody! Are you going to dunk me today?"

The kid nodded and handed over their tickets to the

person collecting them. The ticket taker then handed over three baseballs.

Cody hit on the first one, and Eric splashed down into the tank. Everyone cheered. Melody leaned in close to Zach. "How many times has he gone down?"

Libby tried really hard not to let her mind wander into completely inappropriate directions, considering the setting.

"This is number five. Butter fingers over here couldn't even hit the target once."

Tony winked at Melody. "My talents with my fingers lie in other areas of life."

Melody rolled her eyes and ignored him. "Cody's going to hit all three."

Cody indeed hit all three, and Libby learned that even though the kid was only ten-years-old, scouts were sniffing around them. As Cody and their dad walked away, Melody caught her look and said, "Don't worry. Damien was in the minor leagues after college, and is more worried about Cody being a kid and having fun."

"Hey, Mel. Are you going to take a shot?" Eric called out from the dunking booth after climbing back onto the seat.

Melody grinned back at him. "I want number eleven. Your girlfriend's up next!"

When Melody pushed Libby forward, she realized her friend meant her. She tried not to panic at the use of the word girlfriend, but Eric was smiling at her. Unlike what she was sure was the completely terror-filled expression she was wearing.

Ana came over and took Mayzie's leash. "You need to buy tickets, so we'll hold your place in line. You might want to get a set of twenty because you can use them at other booths. It'll cost you five for a set of three balls here."

"Twenty tickets."

"Yep. A dollar a ticket, so you'll need a twenty-dollar bill."

"I've got one of those."

"Mm-hmm. I've got Mayzie. Go on."

In a daze, Libby went over to where Ana directed her and stood in line to buy her tickets to dunk Eric. Thankfully, she didn't fumble too much when the seller asked for cash.

Back at the dunking booth, she handed over five tickets and got three balls back. Eric grinned at her from the tank, but that just caused her stomach to flip, and it was already flipping enough.

She closed her eyes, took five deep breaths, and then opened her eyes to focus on the target. Pretending the ball was a dart, she drew back and launched it.

Eric yelled.

Bull's eye.

She waited until he stood up in the tank and wiped his face clear of water. "Get back up there. I've got two more balls."

He grinned at her. "I can't wait."

Once he was back up on the seat, she blocked everything out again and focused on the target.

Another bull's eye.

Melody and Ana were cheering, and Tony was laughing as Eric dragged himself back up onto the seat.

She let out a breath, focused on the target, and threw again.

This time, Eric created a big enough splash that all of them—except for Libby—got wet.

"I'm going to get you for that!" Melody put Button back into the wagon and stalked over to the ticket stand.

Eric yelled after her. "I'll be waiting." He looked over at Libby and winked. "I can't wait to hear how you did that."

She opened her mouth, but he shook his head. "Later."

As Melody came back, he held up his wrist and tapped it. "Come on, I don't have all day. I clock out in two minutes."

Melody handed over her tickets, then tossed a ball into the air. "All I need is one."

She was so worked up that she missed the target by a mile with the first ball. The second ball came closer, but still missed.

Growling, she held out the third ball to Libby. "Avenge me."

Eric grinned. "Thirty—"

She launched the last ball and had him falling into the water before he could finish. He came up sputtering and laughing.

Melody jumped and cheered. "Got you! I win!"

She came over and held her hand up for Libby, who high-fived her. Eric rested his arms on the rim of the tank. "You two done cheering?"

Melody went over and danced in front of him, chanting. "I win. I win. I win win win."

Ana came over to Libby and shook her head. "I apologize for the actions of my best friend. She's a little competitive."

Libby smiled. "I can tell."

Eric climbed out of the tank, and a volunteer handed him a towel. He rubbed his face and hair down. With the towel slung across his shoulders and his hair mussed, he looked a lot younger than early thirties.

He walked around Melody, who was still dancing and chanting, and rolled his eyes at Libby. "I'm going to get changed. Where are you headed next?"

She opened her mouth, but no words came out. She cleared her throat. "I don't know." So eloquent.

He must have realized she was feeling awkward as he

just bent down to pet Mayzie, who was sniffing his feet and legs. "How about I meet you at the fried dough booth in fifteen minutes? I've got a change of clothes stashed at the office."

"Okay. What's fried dough?"

That question apparently was enough of a shock that Melody stopped dancing and chanting and came over. "You don't know fried dough?"

"Well, I assume it's like a doughnut or beignet."

"It is not like a doughnut or beignet. We need to fix this ignorance of one of our finest local foods. Get changed, Eric." She made a regal shooing motion and looped her arm through Libby's. "To Kavanaugh's Fried Dough Stand!"

On the way to the stand, Libby learned relatives of her new landlord ran Kavanaugh's Fried Dough Stand. His parents, in fact. The older couple had an efficient operation going. Mrs. Kavanaugh took tickets, five for each serving, and Mr. Kavanaugh produced pillowy deliciousness covered in powdered sugar.

Tony and Zach had followed along with them, and everyone had gotten their own serving. Mayzie calmly sat at Libby's feet as she pulled apart pieces, but was quick to investigate anything that fell from their paper plates.

Eric came over and wrapped an arm around her shoulders before picking a small piece of dough from her plate and popping it into his mouth.

"Hey! That's mine."

He grinned and kissed her cheek. "Thanks."

She wrinkled her nose at him, but he just laughed. "Fine, I'll go get my own. Be right back."

When he returned with his own plate, she reached over and tore off a piece of dough to replace what he'd taken.

They spent the rest of the afternoon hanging out. One end of the street fair was an empty lot where carnival rides had been set up. After he'd found out that she'd never been on carnival rides, even as a kid, Eric convinced her to leave Mayzie with Ana while they worked their way through the more popular ones.

Surprisingly, despite her fear of heights, the Ferris Wheel was her favorite. A view of Lake Ontario spread out before them when they stopped at the top of the ride.

"Can we see Canada?"

Eric laughed. "Probably? I mean, we can't see land, but some of the water is probably on the other side of the border."

He was relaxed in the seat, even as it rocked, with his arm along the back. She took advantage of his position and rested against his side. He moved his arm to her shoulders and squeezed. "How are you doing?"

"Okay? It helps that the ride is going slow and you're here. I definitely would not want to do this alone." Having a gorgeous view to look out on, instead of down at the ground, also helped.

"We're going to get off once we hit the ground, so what do you want to do next?"

She'd seen kids hyped up for one ride that had her curious. "What about that one that spins? The Gravelton?"

He laughed. "Gravitron. How's your stomach?"

"What do you mean?"

"I mean the ride is notorious for making people throw up. Can you handle getting spun around without losing the fried dough?"

Libby thought about it, and while she wasn't sure if she was fully up to it, she'd never gotten carsick or airsick. "Let's do it."

"All right. But if anything happens, you can't say I didn't warn you."

"Warning duly noted."

They got in line, and Melody and Tony joined them. Eric crossed his arms and stared at Melody. "What are you doing here?"

"I want to ride, and this one won't leave me alone?"

Tony held up his hands. "I'm just in line behind you."

"Melody."

Libby looked between them. "What's wrong?"

Eric didn't break the stare as he answered her. "Remember how I said this ride is notorious for making people throw up? This one is notorious for being the one person every year who throws up. I do not want to get thrown up on Melody."

She waved her hand. "Enh. My stomach feels rock solid this year. I am determined to get through at least one ride on it without throwing up."

"Melody. Not this year. Okay?"

Melody stared right back at him, and Libby got the impression there was some kind of silent sibling talk happening because finally she threw up her hands. "Fine. I won't go on."

She headed over to where Ana and Zach stood with the dogs. Ana had Mayzie's leash in hand, but Zach had taken over puppy duty.

Tony continued standing behind them. Eric looked at him. "What about you?"

"I'm just standing in line like I told your sister. Also, I don't throw up. I have a steel-encased stomach."

Libby saw the ride person had opened the gate for people getting off. Quite a few of them had a green tinge to their skin, and a couple stumbled off the ride as if they were drunk.

She felt Eric's gaze on her and looked up. "Are you sure you want to do this?"

Drawing in a deep breath, she nodded.

He reached down and squeezed her hand. "Okay. You get to pick where we stand."

"Is there a space better than the others?"

"Nope. All places are equal on the Gravitron."

The person manning the ride came back out and opened the gate for the new people. Eric handed over the amount of tickets needed for the two of them, and Libby headed for an empty section of wall on the opposite side from the entrance.

She looked around at the wall and saw nothing to buckle in with.

"What are you looking for?"

"Seatbelts?"

Tony laughed and positioned himself a few spaces down from Eric. "No seatbelts on this ride, Libs." He positioned his hands behind his head as if he were lying down on the beach.

Libby looked at Eric. "No seatbelts?"

"Gravity is our seatbelt for this ride." He squeezed her hand, and soon the ride minder came around for one last check. They closed the gate and rock music blasted through speakers near her head.

The ride gathered speed, and the wall behind her lifted. Eric never let go of her hand, even as the wall sections began rising and falling with the movement of the ride. Libby screamed out in joy as she realized gravity kept her plastered against the wall, but moving somewhat freely through space at the whim of whichever pole of gravity was strongest.

After a few minutes, the ride slowed down, and her section of wall slid down until her feet were touching the floor. The ride came to a stop along with the music, and Libby stepped away from the wall.

But without the solid support behind her, her knees

were cooked noodles. She only stayed upright because Eric caught her. Holding onto him, because no way was she going to let pride cause her to face plant in front of him, she made her way off the ride.

When they got back outside, she managed to get enough rigidity back into her knees. Tony, damn him, looked as if he'd gone for a stroll along the beach.

Ana came over with Mayzie, who started whining. Crouching—because that would be a shorter fall if her knees couldn't hold up—she petted her dog. "I'm okay. I promise. Just need to catch my breath."

Eric crouched down as well. "Seriously, are you okay?"

Libby grinned at him. "Yeah. It was fun. But I see your earlier point about upset stomachs."

He began rubbing her back. "Do you need me to get you some ginger ale?"

"No. The stomach's fine. The knees are still feeling a bit weak, though."

He held out his arm. "Come on. Let's head down to the beach so we can stake out a place to have dinner and watch the fireworks."

They had agreed to meet his mom who'd be bringing dinner, and would take the puppies and Mayzie back to the motel before the fireworks started. Their whole group, including Tony and Zach, who they seemed to have absorbed, started making their way through the street fest for the beach.

They stopped at a couple of booths, including one run by a local Amish family selling honey and beeswax items along with handmade quilts. Libby resisted the urge to pet one that was a sunburst of yellows, oranges, and reds.

Eric stroked her back. "Why don't you buy it?"

"It's gorgeous, but I'm sure it's expensive. I just don't

have the cash for this right now. Not with my father doing what he's doing." They moved on.

At one point, Eric said he needed to grab something from the office and he'd meet up with them. They were nearly at the access path to the beach when he did. Mrs. Keller was waiting for them on a spot of beach away from the rest of the crowd, but with easy access to the path, so she'd be able to head out with the dogs later.

They enjoyed the picnic dinner Mrs. Keller had prepared and took turns playing fetch with Mayzie, who enjoyed running into the water for her favorite tennis balls.

When it was time for Mrs. Keller to head out, she kissed each of her children and then hugged Libby. "I can keep the dogs overnight, so don't worry about picking them up later. Stay out as late as you'd like."

"Thank you, Mrs. Keller."

She laughed. "One of these days, I'll get you to call me Nina."

Libby settled back onto the blanket Eric had brought with him from the office. The rest of the group had wandered off to investigate reports of an ice cream truck further down the beach.

"Did you enjoy the Street Fair?"

She nodded. "I did. I know there's stuff like the booths in New York, but my father never took me to anything like it when I was growing up. And certainly not for any carnival rides."

Eric snorted. "I bet not."

Libby shivered as the breeze of the lake wrapped around them.

"Shit. I should have told you to bring a sweater."

"It's nothing."

"Come here." He set his legs apart and pulled her over so that she was seated between them, her back to his chest.

He wrapped his arms around her, and her temperature shot up.

She began shivering for another reason, and he hugged her even tighter. She gripped his thighs where they were exposed by the hem of his shorts. The feel of the taut muscles had her thinking dirty, dirty thoughts. Inappropriate for being out in public at a family event. She had developed a terrible habit of dirty thoughts starring him at inappropriate times.

His breath brushed across her ear. "Libby?"

Libby realized as the first fireworks of the night went off that she didn't want the day with him to end. She turned and brushed her lips against his. "Take me home tonight."

twelve

THE REQUEST SURPRISED ERIC, BUT HE ALSO DIDN'T WANT TO SAY no. Instead of immediately answering, he placed a kiss against the crook of her neck. Libby leaned her head to the side, giving him more access.

Wanting to be explicitly clear, he moved his mouth up to her ear. "Are you sure you want this?"

"Want what?" Her tone was reedy.

"Me kissing you. Whatever happens later."

"Yes."

He pressed another kiss behind her ear. "Just remember, you can always say no. At any point. I'll make sure you get home safe." For as much as he wanted to protect himself, he would never let her come to any harm.

She squeezed his thigh. "Thank you."

He heard Melody's voice carrying on the breeze and looked over to see the rest of their group making their way over to them, ice cream cones in hand. No one said anything about Libby's change in position, and Libby didn't move away from him. They stayed like that through the fireworks show.

He'd always loved the Start of Summer Street Fair's

closing fireworks show. It had meant the true start of summer when he was a kid. As an adult, he'd enjoyed the nostalgia. But now, he knew the feel of Libby's body against his would be seared into his memory. No future fireworks show could live up to it.

After the show was over, they gathered up what his mom had left and headed back to the office where he and Melody had parked their cars. Zach and Caputo walked back with him.

When he looked at Zach, the other man briefly shrugged. "Habit. I like to make sure the rest of my team is settled for the night."

He had a flashback to when they'd been in high school, and Zach had been one of the football team's captains. He hadn't been the one hyping them all up, but he had been the one ensuring no one had done anything truly stupid. At the time, he claimed that he was the only one allowed to do stupid shit.

When they were at the back of the office, Zach and Caputo peeled off. He waited until Melody and Ana were squared away and off in her truck before he started his own.

He looked over at Libby again. "I can take you back to the motel to pick up the dogs and your car."

She let out a breath and then shook her head. "No. I appreciate you giving me the opportunity, but I want to go home with you."

He nodded and put his truck in gear. Twenty minutes later, thanks to the congestion of everyone leaving the show at the same time, they were walking into his home.

Looking at the space through Libby's eyes, he winced. He was a bachelor who was building a new business. He also hadn't expected to have company tonight. The place wasn't a total disaster, but it also could have been more presentable.

"Sorry."

Libby laughed. "About what?"

He waved his hand around. "I would have cleaned up if I'd known you were coming over."

Libby turned to him and pressed a kiss against his jaw. "Eric, I'd been living in a motel room with a dog and five puppies, and living in our own house hasn't actually gotten much better. Believe me, this is fine."

He lowered his jaw until their lips were touching. He pressed his to hers and let himself sink into the feeling of hers. Silky and warm. Raising his hands, he cupped her face and tilted it for a better angle.

She moaned and opened her mouth. She deserved gentle, but he wanted to ravish her. Stake claim to her.

Which made him little better than her father. He worked to throttle back the caveman instincts and slowly released his grip on her face.

Her eyes blinked open. "What?"

"Upstairs. You deserve better than a couch."

She smiled and traced a finger around his lips. He shuddered at the touch. She could enthrall him easily, and he wasn't sure he wanted to resist.

"Okay. Which way?"

He led her up to his bedroom. The upstairs only had two rooms besides the bathroom. His bedroom and a room he'd turned into his office. Thankfully, he didn't have piles of laundry strewn across his bed. But he also hadn't bothered to make it this morning. Deciding it was easier to just strip it, he pulled all the bedding off and tossed it into the space between the bed and the wall.

Libby laughed, and it was sunlight breaking through clouds. She came over and placed her hands on the waistband of his shorts, underneath the shirt he'd changed into earlier. "Impatient?"

He ran his hands up and down her arms. "Maybe a little. I don't want to worry about it later."

She pressed a kiss at the base of his throat. "I like that. Speaking of worry. Do you have condoms?"

"Yeah, but let me check the expiration date."

He let her go long enough to run into the bathroom where he'd stored them the last time he went on a cleaning frenzy. Thankfully, the date was still good, but barely.

Taking a couple in hand, he headed back into the bedroom to find Libby on the bed, dressed only in her bra and panties.

He opened his mouth to say something, but nothing came out. She leaned back against the headboard and brushed one hand over the swell of her breast. "I was feeling a little impatient myself. I had some inappropriate thoughts earlier today when we were out in public."

"Okay." As he walked over to the bed, he pulled his shirt over his head and tossed it in the corner. "Want to share them?"

Her eyes darkened as she looked him over. He tossed the condoms onto the bed and sat down by her hip.

She turned toward him, and he couldn't resist the opportunity to run his hand along her thigh, up over her hip, and to her breast.

"I like that."

"What were you thinking of earlier, Libby?"

She molded her hand around his, increasing the pressure against her breast, even as she arched into his grip. "When we were at the dunk tank, Melody asked how many times you'd gone down."

His laugh, when it came, was rough. "Want me to go down on you, Libby?"

"Yes. I don't always come. And it helps."

"Okay. Anything else I should know?"

"I've only been with a few guys."

"That's fine. What have you done to yourself that you like?"

Libby closed her eyes even as she moved her hand down and cupped her mound through her panties. "I play with myself."

"Um-hmm." He bent and licked a line up from the hollow of her throat to her lower jaw. Lightly bit her there. "What else?"

"I've got a vibrator."

He moved his hand from her breast to cup his hand over hers. "Do you like it?" He squeezed.

She gasped. "Yes."

"How many batteries do you go through in a month?"

Her eyelids fluttered open. "What do you mean?"

"I mean..." He kissed her deeply, even as he began a rhythmic squeezing with his hand until she gasped and broke the kiss. "How often do you use your vibrator? How many batteries do you go through?"

"Oh." Her laugh was breathless. "I don't use batteries."

He lifted his head and looked at her until she met his gaze. But he didn't stop playing with her panty-covered core. "You have a vibrator that doesn't use batteries?"

"Uh-huh. It plugs in."

It was his turn to blink. "Damn." He quickly recalculated his plan of attack. "Do you need it to come?" He wasn't sure where he could get a vibrator at this time of night if she needed one.

She wrapped her free hand around his neck and pulled him down. "No. But I need you to give me a bit more attention."

He grinned. "I have no problems with that."

They kissed some more, and she removed her hand from under his so that the only thing separating him from where he was looking forward to spending some quality time was her panties. He slipped his fingers under the fabric and pushed it down a little. She helped until her panties were down at her knees.

He stroked the soft skin and the hair covering it. She sighed and let her legs fall open as far as the panties would allow. When he dipped his fingers down and along her slit, he felt wetness, but not a lot.

Breaking the kiss, he lifted his head. "Lube?"

"It would help."

"Okay. Don't move. Be right back." He got off the bed and ran to the bathroom. He grabbed the lube he'd stashed with the condoms and brought it back to the bed. She'd fully removed her panties and her bra and tossed them on top of the rest of her clothes.

He sat down on the bed and dribbled a little on his fingers before putting them back where he'd enjoyed having them.

Libby yelped a little when he touched her outer lips, near her clit. "Sorry."

She shook her head. "I forgot how cool it can feel."

He bent down and gave her a quick kiss. "Still with me?"

"Yeah. How about you take off your shorts?"

His dick would like to know the answer to that, too. "I'll leave them on for a bit. No need to rush."

He moved the lube around her lower lips. She splayed out one leg, and he moved one finger to enter her.

Libby felt like heaven. He listened to her as he pressed kisses down her throat to her breasts. Her nipples had tightened up, and he kissed first one, then the other. She let out a soft moan, so he sucked the second nipple into his mouth and bit down a little. Her hips bucked, driving his finger deeper into her.

"Eric."

Definitely a winning combination. He began a rhythm of sucking on her breast in time to the movement of his finger in her. After a bit, he slid a second finger in and placed his thumb next to her clit.

She moved her hands to his head and threaded her fingers into his hair. His hair wasn't long, but she got a good grip on him.

When he began softly stroking his thumb over her clit, she pulled tighter on his head. He lightly bit down again, and felt the squeeze of her inner muscles. God, it would feel so good once he could get his dick in her. But first, she needed to come.

He released her breast and moved his head so he could shower some love on the other one. He didn't stop pumping his fingers, and after a few minutes, he felt her inner muscles tighten even harder around them.

Letting go of her breast, he moved over her and down, replacing his thumb with his lips and tongue.

"Eric?"

"You still okay?" He looked up to meet her gaze.

She had pushed up on her elbows. She had a dazed look in her eyes, and her hair was mussed from moving around on his bed. "Are you sure?"

What the hell kind of man had she been with before? Obviously, her ex-fiancè hadn't done it for her, or she would now be married to him. "Yeah. What about you?"

"If you're sure."

"I am." He put emphasis on his surety by kissing her clit.

Libby moaned, and he felt her flop back onto the bed. Without moving his head, he reached out with his freehand and located one of his pillows. Encouraging her to lift her hips, he stuffed it under them.

With the better angle, he maneuvered a third finger into her. She once again gripped his head. When she tried to direct him, he followed and was rewarded with her hips bucking again. This time, he curled his fingers so that the tips dragged against the upper wall of her vagina.

Her body began shaking, and she held his face tight to her pussy. He released the suction on her clit and began lightly licking her until he felt the crest of the orgasm pass. When her body relaxed, he gave her clit one more kiss, and moved back up her body.

Laying next to her, his fingers resting inside her, he pressed a kiss to her shoulder.

She turned her head and pulled him to meet her lips. He lost himself in the kiss and the feel of her lips.

Libby released his head to push at his shoulders, and he moved to lie on his back...and almost fell off the bed.

He laughed as they both scrambled to stop the fall. The bottle of lube, and probably both the condoms, fell to the floor. He managed to get a foot on the floor, but the angle caused a cramp in his quad.

Wincing, he grabbed the edge of the mattress to pull himself back up.

"Eric? Are you okay?"

"Yeah, just a cramp. I'll walk it out."

"Oh my God. I'm so sorry." Libby started to get up from the bed, but he gripped her upper arms.

"It's okay. I'm okay. Just give me a moment." He walked around the room, pausing to pick up the condoms and lube.

She flopped back onto the bed and covered her face. "How the hell do I ruin things every time?"

He paused. That was not the reaction he was expecting. Sometimes sex was sweet. Sometimes it was dirty. He loved the dirty bits. And sometimes it was downright hilarious. This was one of the hilarious times.

"Libby?"

She rolled away from him. Yeah. Not good.

He sat down next to her, stretching his one leg out to get rid of the last of the cramp, and placed his hand on her shoulder.

She pushed her hair away from her face. "You want me to leave, right?"

"What? No. No."

"Do you want to have sex now?"

Who the hell had fucked her head up so much about sex? Whoever they were deserved to get taken out behind the bleachers and beat down. And then forced to attend a sex ed class focused on making sure you pleasured your partner.

"Only if you want to, but you don't seem to be in the right headspace at the moment."

She screwed up her face. "I want to."

He looked at her for a few seconds. "Yeah...that's not a convincing answer. Come on. I'll get you the robe Mom got me a few Christmases ago, and we'll go down and watch a movie."

"I should just go home."

Eric thought about it for a moment. She said she should go home, not that she wanted to go home. He wanted to make sure she didn't wallow over this. If she truly wanted to go home, he'd take her home, but he thought hanging out with him in a low pressure setting would be a lot better for whatever future they might have.

"If you absolutely want to go back home, I'll take you back. But I'd love it if you stayed the night. No more sex. Because what we've already done? That was totally sex."

She blew out a breath. "Okay. But I get to pick the movie."

Please let her be into action adventure because that's

what he had stored on his DVR. "Sure. And if I don't have it, I can get it from one of those rental services. Just give me a second to grab the robe."

He had to go digging into the clothes boxes he kept stored in the office closet, but he finally unearthed the robe in the third box. When he brought it back to her, he found Libby had put her bra and panties back on.

He held out the robe to her. She smiled a little and got it wrapped around her. "I think I've got some packets of microwave popcorn in the kitchen. You up for it?"

"Sure. Thanks."

He reached out and pushed a lock of hair behind her ear. Tipped her chin up with a finger. "Hey. It's going to be okay. Seriously." He bent down and pressed a kiss against her lips. After a few moments, she softened against him, and her hands came up to rest against his hips. They kept kissing. When his dick began getting impatient about moving the action back to the bed, he broke it.

Both of them were breathing heavily, so he took the moment to grab a fresh t-shirt from his dresser. Then he took hold of her hand and led her back downstairs.

After finding a popcorn packet and tossing it into his microwave, he headed back into the living room to find her settled on the couch. He opened the storage ottoman and pulled out a blanket his grandma had crocheted for him as a kid. "Here. I don't have a lot of blankets, but this should be big enough that we can share it."

She smiled at him and took it. "Thanks."

"Do you want anything to drink? I've got beer, a couple cans of pop."

"Considering how late it is, water's fine."

"All right. Do you want anything on your popcorn?"

"Do you have Milk Duds?"

He made an exaggerated wince. "I was hoping you'd

just say butter and salt."

She laughed, and it made him feel better. If he could make her laugh, they should be good.

"Butter and salt are fine."

He headed back into the kitchen and grabbed one of the mixing bowls his mom used when she was over. After dumping the only slightly burned popcorn into it, he melted some butter, and then tossed that on with some salt. He poured a large cup of water for her and grabbed a beer for himself.

Back in the living room, he flipped the top of the ottoman to turn it into a tray, situated it in front of them, and then got the TV started.

"What do you want to watch?"

"The Notebook?"

He swallowed and opened the search function before he realized she'd started laughing at him. Laughing so hard that she had fallen on her side and was rolling around on the couch.

Sending her a grumpy glare, he began selecting the letters to search for it. "I should make you watch it as revenge."

"No. No. Ten Things I Hate About You. Please." She somehow squeaked out the words between bouts of laughter.

Not an action adventure movie, but Heath Ledger. He searched for it, brought it up, and then tossed the remotes onto the tray.

Libby sat up and tossed part of the blanket over his lap. He stretched his arm around her shoulders, and they settled in to watch Kat and Bianca send the guys of Padua High into tailspins.

He had never been in more complete sympathy for them in his life.

thirteen

THE NEXT MORNING, LIBBY FLOPPED DOWN ON HER BED. SHE hadn't retrieved Mayzie and the puppies from Mrs. Keller yet. She wasn't sure how she could face the woman after spending the night with Eric.

Even if they hadn't fully had sex.

Despite what Eric said, she knew something was missing. Even if spending most of the night cuddled up next to him while movies played was more intimate than she'd ever been with the other men she'd slept with.

Not even Herman, her ex-fiancè, had truly known her despite the fact that they'd spent time together off and on since childhood.

Every other man she'd been with had been more about the physical connection rather than the emotional. Whenever there'd been an event like what had happened with Eric, they'd just left until the next time they got together. Not one of them had comforted or commiserated with her.

It was obvious she needed a better quality boyfriend.

Her phone rang from where she'd plugged it in.

It was tempting to leave it there while she brooded on

the bed, but in case it was Eric, she didn't want him worrying about her.

After getting up, she saw it wasn't Eric, but Greer. For half a second, she allowed letting it go to voicemail to tempt her, but Greer would also be worried with everything else going on.

But she'd let it ring too long, and it switched to voicemail as soon as she picked up her phone. She immediately opened her contacts list and hit the call button.

It rang a couple times before Greer switched to answering the call. "Hey. Are you doing okay?"

Libby headed back to the bed and flopped down. "Okay. Mostly."

"Why only mostly?"

She could hear the frown in Greer's tone. "How about I call you back in a bit? I need to pick up Mayzie, and I want to take her to this place I know."

"Not the puppies? Are they adopted out already?"

"No, but they're getting close. Where I want to go is not puppy friendly, and I'd be way too distracted by them wanting to run everywhere to concentrate on talking with you. I can at least trust Mayzie not to wander too far from me."

"Okay. How long? I'm headed to Nana's for Sunday dinner in a couple hours."

"About half an hour?"

"Sounds good."

Libby signed off and began gathering what she'd need for going to the field. Picking up a couple of Mayzie's balls from her toy chest, she also remembered to fill a water bottle. She wasn't sure if the creek water was good, and didn't want Mayzie drinking from it just in case.

When she walked into the motel's office about fifteen minutes later, Mrs. Keller was helping a young Asian couple check in. She waved at Libby, but continued going through the spiel of the local attractions. The young man wandered over to the display of brochures, while the young woman asked Mrs. Keller some questions.

She soon got them situated and came around the counter once they were gone. She gave Libby a big hug. "Did you have fun last night?"

Libby's mind completely blanked. No way in hell was Mrs. Keller asking if she had *fun* with Eric, but all Libby could think of was how he looked going down on her.

She finally scraped together syllables. "Yes. Had fun."

Mrs. Keller laughed. "I hope you're not dealing with a hangover this morning? I know all my kids can tie one on."

"No. Just a little out of sorts." To say the least. "I was wondering if I could leave the puppies with you for a little longer? I want to take Mayzie out for a walk in the woods."

"Of course. Melody's working in the office today, so I can leave Button and the others with her if I need to take care of things."

"Thank you."

Mrs. Keller went into the private apartment attached to the office, and came back out with Mayzie already wearing her harness. Mayzie bounded over to her, jumped up, and began licking at her.

"It's good to see you, too, Mayz." Libby hooked her hand into the loop of the leash. "Are you ready for a walk?"

Mayzie headed for the door, tugging hard on the leash. Mrs. Keller laughed again. "You two have fun. The puppies are fine here as long as you need them to be."

"Thank you. I don't know what I'd do without your help."

Mrs. Keller winked. "That's what being a good neighbor means. When someone needs help, and you can provide, you do that. Go on."

Libby got Mayzie settled in the back seat of Greer's car, and pulled out of the lot. She was passing the diner when she realized she was hungry. Eric had made them breakfast this morning, but she hadn't fully appreciated it with her stomach still tied up in knots over what had happened the night before.

A parking spot opened up across the street from the diner, so she quickly pulled in. She left Mayzie in the car with the windows down and hurried across the street. This time it was Lydia who took her take out order. While she waited, she stepped back outside so she could keep an eye on Mayzie. The dog had her head out the window and made it clear she was watching where Libby went.

She laughed. She didn't know what she would have done the last few weeks if it weren't for Mayzie and the puppies. Thankfully, she didn't have to wait long, and saw Lydia waving at her from the welcome stand. She went in and grabbed her lunch.

Back on the road with Mayzie, she did her best to follow the roads Eric had taken when they'd gone up to his uncle's private land. She hoped he wouldn't be mad that she was headed up there to have a private conversation with Greer. She'd gotten the impression that where he'd taken her had been his secret. One he'd shared with her.

Her memory held, and she was soon turning down the road Eric had turned onto. She parked in the same spot he had and got all the stuff she'd brought with her out of the car before letting Mayzie loose.

Mayzie was good and stuck by her until she found a comfortable spot to spread out the blanket she'd brought with.

Once she got settled, she propped up her phone and started a video call with Greer. Her friend answered after a couple of rings. From the background, she was walking around Manhattan.

"There you are."

Mayzie recognized Greer's voice and sniffed at the phone, blocking the camera.

"And there's Mayzie. Hi, baby girl. Where are your babies?"

Mayzie let out a woof and then settled down when she realized Greer wasn't there to give her pets.

Libby laughed. "I left them with Mrs. Keller."

"Where are you?"

"Hold on." Libby picked up the phone, switched the view, and scanned the horizon. "Don't tell Eric, but this is his uncle's land. He brought me here a couple of weeks ago. I probably shouldn't be showing you this."

"Damn. That's a gorgeous view. My lips are sealed. Speaking of Eric. What's going on, Libs? Did something happen?"

Libby reversed the view and put the phone back where she'd propped it up. "Mind if I eat my lunch?"

Even through the sunglasses her friend wore, Libby could see the narrowing of her eyes. "Libby?"

"I'm hungry."

"You're stalling."

Mayzie barked.

"See. Even your dog agrees with me."

Libby stuck her tongue out at Mayzie. "Traitor."

"Did you sleep with Eric last night?"

Libby winced. "Kind of?"

"What kind of answer is kind of?"

"It's the 'we started to have sex, and I freaked the fuck out' answer."

Greer's video bounced as if she'd tripped. "What?"

"Please don't tell me you have me on speaker in public?"

"No. I hate assholes who do that. I'm just shocked. Hold on."

Libby watched as buildings flashed through Greer's background until trees and a white stone building with arched windows near the roof line suddenly appeared. "Where are you?"

"Bryant Park. I'm grabbing a table. Okay. I'm no longer in danger of tripping. Tell me everything."

"We hung out yesterday during the street fair and then went to the fireworks show."

Greer's brows waggled. "And were there fireworks?"

Even though her only company was Mayzie, Libby felt a deep blush spread across her cheeks and down her throat. "There were for me. Not so much for him."

"What? He suddenly lost lift? Does he need a little blue pill?"

"No! No. I already told you I freaked out. We were moving on to the next portion of the program when he fell off the bed."

Greer clapped her hand to her mouth. "Oh my God. Did you have to take him to the ER? Is he okay?"

"Greer. Let me finish, will you?"

"Okay. Lips sealed." She pantomimed zipping them.

"He caught himself, but he got a cramp in his thigh. He was working it out, but I had flashbacks to more than a few of my not-so-shining moments with lovers and had a complete meltdown. After he calmed me down, we watched movies while eating popcorn." She rubbed her forehead as she thought again of how humiliating everything had been.

Greer was silent. Then she popped her sunglasses to the

top of her head. "I'm going to be honest here, Libs. I don't see what the problem is."

"I told you. I had a meltdown."

"Which he responded to in a really kind manner, and then you watched movies with him. This is not a problem. If he kicked you out while you were still having the meltdown, then I'd be having words with him."

"You don't understand."

Greer let out a long sigh. "No. I don't. Is it the meltdown that you're worried about?"

"Yes. I ruin everything." Libby felt tears start rolling down her cheeks, and Mayzie sat up. Began licking her face. She pushed the dog away. "Not now, Mayzie."

Mayzie whined. Then barked. Then whined again.

"I get it, Mayzie. Our friend here is just having an existential crisis. Sit down, and put your head on her thigh so she can pet you while we work this out."

Libby laughed when Mayzie did exactly that and then looked up at her when she didn't immediately begin petting her.

"Are you sure you don't want Mayzie when I'm done fostering?"

Mayzie let out a low growl.

"Don't worry, Mayzie. I've got it covered. Libs, you, my friend, are what's known as a foster fail. Mayzie's yours. And you are hers. You'd better get used to it."

Libby froze for a moment when she realized how deeply Greer's words hit her. Her inner self went, "What she said."

"I can't think about that right now." And she couldn't. One existential crisis at a time. Even if claiming Mayzie as hers felt absolutely right down to her bones. "Back on track, Greer."

"Maybe that's what you need, Libs."

She shook her head as she tried to follow her friend's thought patterns. "What do I need?"

"To get off track. All your tracks. You had bad to not great experiences with lovers before, so of course your brain codes this the same way. That's what I'm telling you. Your feelings are absolutely valid, but they're not always reality. Especially when the only person telling you that things aren't right is yourself. What did Eric say last night?"

"Not much. When I asked if he wanted me to leave, he said I could if I wanted to, but he didn't think I actually wanted to. When I offered to have sex, he declined because he didn't think I was in the right headspace."

"Sounds like you weren't."

She rubbed her forehead with the hand that wasn't petting Mayzie. "Probably. But why did he offer to watch movies with me?"

"Because it sounds like he's a truly good guy and didn't want you to go home and stew over what happened. This is simple, Libs. He wouldn't have asked you to stay if he didn't care about you on some level. Go talk to him. I'm not the person you need to talk to most about this."

"But you're who I trust."

"Which, honey, I love you for that, but you need to learn to trust men more, and it sounds like you can trust Eric."

"That's my problem, isn't it?"

"What?"

"That I don't trust men."

"Yeah, I'm honestly amazed that you've even dated, let alone had sex. With everything your dad has done to control your life, there's not a solid foundation for building trust."

Libby flopped back on the ground before realizing she kicked her phone over.

"Why am I suddenly seeing the sky? Are you okay?"

She scrambled to right herself and then picked up the phone. "Sorry. I just hate that you're right."

"I'm not a fan of myself at the moment, either. Do you need me to come up to Sunflower Falls?"

Libby sighed. "No. Thanks. I should be okay. I'll call Eric and see if we can meet up. Thanks for listening to me."

"Thanks for calling me. Getting all up in your head about this isn't good for you, or fair to Eric. Honestly, I think it's time you saw a therapist about this."

Libby's lips twisted. "I'll put it on my list."

"While you're at it, call Mr. Billings first thing tomorrow. I talked with him on Friday, and it sounded like there might be some movement."

"Thanks. I will. Have fun at your Nana's."

Greer scowled. "Honestly, I'm tempted to drive up to Sunflower Falls to avoid it. My aunt's in town."

"Which one?"

"Hetta. I think she's divorcing husband number four."

Libby winced. Greer's aunt, her mother's sister, ran through husbands faster than entire wardrobes. She'd become famous in her early twenties as a model and had gone through a string of famous lovers and husbands ever since. And when she was home, she always needled Greer about her single status. "I'm sure Mrs. Keller can find you a room."

Greer blew out a breath. "I'll keep the option open. If Hetta's on a roll, I'm sure I can get Kimmy to drive up with me."

"Text me later tonight."

"Will do. Go talk with Eric. Bye, Mayzie."

Mayzie woofed goodbye, and Libby ended the call. She looked out at the view. It was nice and quiet up here. The perfect location for contemplating the state of your life. Greer wasn't wrong.

She probably did need to go see a therapist. But she also needed to review a couple of appearance contracts that Greer had forwarded Friday night for another one of their clients. Some things just took priority.

"And talking with Eric should be at the top of my to-do list. Right, Mayz?"

Mayzie's answer was to root around in the bag containing her takeout from the diner.

"No. That's not for you." Libby yanked the bag away to the other side of her body.

Mayzie sighed and rolled over onto her back. Libby began rubbing her exposed belly. "Fine. You get pets. How about you go explore while I eat, and then we'll head back to town?"

Mayzie woofed and scrambled up. She headed out toward the creek, sniffing all the flowers and more.

Libby kept an eye on her while she ate. Mayzie never went too far, and didn't splash around too much in the creek. She was not a fan of baths.

After Libby finished her sandwich, she called over to Mayzie, who trotted back. Libby poured a cup of water for her, and she hurriedly slurped it down.

Gathering up everything she'd brought with from the car, she looped Mayzie's leash around her wrist. "Come on. Let's head back so I can call Eric."

They drove back to town, and Libby parked in the mostly empty motel parking lot. She was glad she'd taken the time to talk with Greer. She felt a lot more settled, and hadn't realized how badly she needed that.

Since she had some privacy for the moment, she took the time to call Eric.

It rang a couple of times. "Yeah?"

"Hey Eric. It's Libby."

"You okay?"

She chewed on her lip. "Let's just say that I'm better than I was last night."

"I'm glad to hear it."

"I also wanted to thank you."

"What for?"

"For not making me feel any worse than I did. I know that must not have been easy."

"Look, Libby..." She waited for him to say something, but he only sighed. "I don't know what kind of guy you've been with before, but anyone who made you feel bad if something didn't go...I guess right's the best word...when you were intimate with them was an asshole. Shit goes wrong all the time. Sometimes during sex. That's life. You roll with it. And if someone doesn't, that's their problem, not yours. Got me?"

He surprised a laugh out of her with how adamant he was. "Yeah. Thank you."

"Listen. I'm supposed to meet up with Zach and Caputo later. How about we try for dinner tomorrow? Does that work for you?"

"Where?"

"My place. How do you feel about me getting a sitter for Mayzie and the puppies?"

Libby petted Mayzie, who'd rested her head on the console. "That sounds great. Mayzie and I left the puppies with your mom, so I should probably get them back together. She hasn't quite weaned them yet, but I think she's getting close."

"Okay. I'll touch base with you tomorrow."

"Bye, Eric."

His voice, when he responded, was deliciously husky. "Bye, Libby."

Libby hung up and let out a long breath. Mayzie lifted

her head. "I think I might have actually found a good guy. Hopefully, I won't fuck it up."

Her phone pinged with an incoming text. Thinking it was Greer, she checked it. Instead, it was from Mr. Billings, asking her if she could call him immediately.

She opened the contact and started a call. He picked up right away. "Hi, Mr. Billings. What's wrong?"

"Liberty. When was the last time you saw or spoke to your father?"

She frowned. "Officially? He came over to my apartment the morning of the bachelorette party. That night, I heard him talking with Herman, but I didn't *see* him."

"So you haven't seen him in the last week?"

She frowned. "No."

"Are you still in Sunflower Falls, or did you return to the city?"

"I'm still in Sunflower Falls. What's going on?"

He sighed. "There's been an emergency motion filed with your father stating you need to be immediately delivered into protective care."

"What?"

"He states that he's been in contact with you, and you are not mentally fit."

"I have not been in contact with him."

Mr. Billings was quiet for a few moments before he responded. "I believe this is a maneuver to draw you out. I will, of course, immediately respond that, as your representative, I am in contact with you, and I am assured of your safety. You may have to appear before the court, but I will do my best to block that."

Libby chewed on her thumbnail. "What about my trust? Can you have him removed as a trustee?"

Mr. Billings' response had her thinking of sharks circling

prey. "Believe me, I'm fully investigating his financial dealings and everything related to the oversight of your trust accounts. Unfortunately, I believe there might be something shady going on, but I don't have specific evidence as yet."

"Thank you, Mr. Billings."

"I'm sorry I don't have better news for you, Liberty."

She let out a sigh. "You can't help it. Have a good day."

She ended the call and looked at Mayzie. "I can't trust my father, but I can trust Eric. I just need to keep telling myself until I believe it. Come on. Let's go get your puppies."

As she headed to the office, Libby realized it was time to put a new plan in place for her life.

fourteen

ERIC PARKED HIS TRUCK AND SHIFTED THE GEAR INTO PARK. Geraghty's was on the outskirts of town where they had enough space for a decently large parking lot. He'd spotted Zach's SUV parked near the entrance when he'd pulled in. As far as he could tell, Caputo let Zach drive him everywhere.

Come to think of it, he'd never seen Caputo out and about without Zach. And he had the distinct impression that it was Caputo who was the one behind them being out. He brushed off the thought and climbed out of his truck.

Just in time to see Sam pull into the lot. He waited for his friend to park before heading over.

Sam also drove a truck, but his was about two decades old and had dirt and other things lining the undercarriage from visiting the various farms.

"Eric. What are you doing here?" Sam held out his hand, and they did the half-handshake, half-hug thing.

"I'm meeting up with Zach Troy and his friend Tony Caputo."

"Nice. I've seen Zach around town a couple times, but haven't had time to catch up."

"Are you meeting anyone?"

"No. Just thought I'd grab a couple beers and dinner. Didn't feel like cooking for myself tonight."

They began walking to the entrance. "Why don't you join us? We're just hanging out."

"That'd be good. Thanks."

Eric was first to the door, so he pulled it open and held it for Sam. The light inside Geraghty's was low, and—despite indoor smoking being banned since before he'd been born—the place gave off the faint scent of crushed cigarettes and cigars. Toward the back, past a couple of pool tables, he spotted movement and realized it was Zach waving his arm.

He tapped Sam on his upper arm and pointed. "There they are." Sam nodded and followed him to the back.

There was a pitcher of beer and a basket of onion rings already on the table.

Zach stood and held out his hand to Sam. "Hey, man. Good to see you."

Caputo remained sitting, but he waved at Sam. "Hey. You're the vet, right?"

Sam nodded as he sat down in one of the empty chairs. "I am. Never caught what you do."

Caputo's smile was amiable as he lifted his glass. "Not much if I can help it."

Zach snorted and then took a swallow of his own drink. "Harry should be around in a couple of minutes. We told him we were going to wait to order food until you got here."

Eric picked up one of the onion rings. "Good of him to bring the onion rings."

Zach stabbed his thumb in Caputo's direction. "That's on him. He wouldn't stop whining."

"You're the one who told me these were world famous. I

had to try them." He patted his stomach. "I've got to stay fit and trim for the ladies."

That had them all laughing, and they relaxed into their seats. Harry soon came around with another glass and pitcher of beer. Since everyone but Caputo knew the menu by heart as it had barely changed in the fifty years Geraghty's had been open, they put in their orders. Caputo walked back to the bar with Harry so Harry could give him one of the few menus that were left.

Eric looked at Zach. "What's his deal?"

Zach shook his head. "He's between gigs essentially right now."

Sam put his glass back down on the table. "I heard he served with you in the Marines."

Zach laughed. "Hell, no. Tony's a good guy, but he is not Marine material. And he'd be the first to tell you that. No. We became friends after I got out. He was looking for a change, and basically hitched a ride when I decided to come home for a bit."

Eric studied Zach as he sipped his own beer. There was something about that story that sounded fine on the surface, but he couldn't put his finger on exactly what about it was bothering him.

Before he could get too deep into his own personal conspiracy theory, Caputo came back and sat down. He let out a long sigh. "You owe me, Zach."

Zach's brows rose, but that was his only reaction. "What for?"

"There is no place around here that believes in serving green goddess dressing. And the only salad I can get here is the house salad."

"Told you that you'd have to make your own."

"Green goddess, Zach. Every place knows how to make it these days."

Zach looked around the table. "Has Harry changed the menu since he bought the place from his dad twenty years ago?"

Both Eric and Sam replied. "Nope."

"And did his dad change the menu in the thirty years he owned the place?"

Again, they answered in synch. "Nope."

Zach turned back to Caputo. "And what makes you think that a dive bar on the shores of Lake Ontario that hasn't changed its menu in over fifty years would serve green goddess dressing?"

Caputo mumbled under his breath and poured himself another beer.

Zach snorted and turned back to Eric. "What's going on with you?"

"What makes you think there's anything going on with me?" He took a long sip of his beer.

"Because I saw you driving off with Libby toward your house last night instead of in the other direction to the motel where she had told me she'd parked her car. You do not have the look of a man who got laid last night."

Sam looked at him so fast, beer sloshed over the rim of his glass onto the table. "You're with Libby?"

"Shout that for the entire bar to hear you, why don't you?"

Sam flipped him the bird. "What crawled up your ass?"

What had happened last night between him and Libby was just between them. She didn't deserve to become barroom gossip.

"Nothing. It's fine." Except...he wasn't sure exactly how to deal with Libby. Patience, yeah. But he felt like he was stumbling around in the dark. And he didn't have Uncle Stef available to give him advice.

He looked around. They were the only ones in this part

of the bar. Maybe he could give them just enough information to help him figure out how to handle things without getting into specific details.

Caputo knocked on the table. "I hereby call to order the Men's Club of Sunflower Falls. Nothing shared beyond this table."

Eric stared at him. "Who are you?"

Caputo saluted him with his beer. "Just your friendly neighborhood slacker."

Eric narrowed his eyes. "Slacker? You just bought property, and put down a deposit for tearing down the house on the property and building a new house."

Caputo waved his finger. "Out of order. We're here to discuss your issues. So, you took the lovely Libby home last night. Is there something about the experience you need advice on?"

Eric rolled his eyes. "No. I'm not going into details about last night."

Zach leaned in so his forearms rested on the table. "But there is something you do want to talk about."

"Yeah. I think it relates to last night, but I'm not sure."

"So something did—or is it didn't—happen last night?" Caputo popped another onion ring into his mouth.

"Ignoring last night, Libby's got some issues with her dad. I don't know all the details, but he filed for guardianship."

Zach's brows rose. "Want me to take care of things?"

Eric laughed and shook his head. "No. I get the impression that her dad's something of a big deal in legal stuff."

Sam tapped his fingers against his glass. "Wasn't Libby engaged, too? I remember her wearing a big diamond ring when you first brought Mayzie and the puppies in."

"Yeah. Turns out her dad was behind that. Her ex apparently ran off with his secretary the morning of the wedding, and everyone thinks Libby's in hiding because she was jilted."

"And she's not?"

"No. She was the one who headed out of town first. And that was because she overheard her dad basically forcing her ex to marry her."

Zach held up his hand, and they quieted as Harry came over with their orders and another pitcher of beer. Once Harry headed back, Zach looked at him. "Her dad sounds like a real piece of work. You sure you don't want me to deal with him?"

"No. Libby's got a lawyer to handle the court stuff, and her partner assured me that the guy they hired is not only the best but also is not a fan of Libby's dad."

Zach cut his burger in half. "Okay, so the legal stuff's taken care of. What's your issue?"

"Between her dad and the guys she's been with in the past, I don't think Libby's the most trusting person. Let's just say that things didn't go as smoothly as they could have, and she was ready to run back home."

"Did you drive her home?" Caputo picked up one of his fries and bit into it.

"We stayed up watching movies because I didn't want her to be by herself."

Zach frowned. "Why?"

Eric thought about how he wanted to phrase things and picked up one of his fries as he picked out his words. "She was blaming herself for things that were no one's fault. Shit happens, you know?"

They all nodded. Caputo picked up another fry, and used it to point at Eric. "And that's when you hug your partner, and cuddle the rest of the night."

Not exactly how Eric would have phrased it, but the sentiment was the same. "I guess I'm not sure how to make it clear to her we're good. I'd like another chance, and not have things go sideways."

They finished the rest of their meal without anyone coming up with any good ideas. Finally, Zach stood up. "Come on."

Eric looked at him over the rim of his glass. "What?"

"Pool. I think better when I'm planning shots."

After a particularly nasty brawl ten years ago, Harry had locked up the cues and balls in the office, so Eric went over to the bar to ask for them. Harry eyed him, and looked over to where Zach, Sam, and Caputo were talking next to the pool table.

"No busting each other up."

"Come on, Harry. Does it look like we're ready to fight?"

"No. But pool fucks with some guys."

"We are not betting, or doing anything else. I promise."

Harry just grunted and finished pouring beers before heading into the office and getting a set of cues and the balls. He handed them to Eric and gave him the beady eye. "No betting."

"I promise."

He headed back to the table and handed the cues to Zach. "I promised Harry no betting."

Zach shrugged. "Wasn't planning on it. I heard he had some issues a couple of weeks back with some guys visiting the area."

"Great." Eric picked out a striped and a solid from the box and rolled them down to the end of the table closest to where they'd been sitting.

Zach handed out the cues. "Tony, you and me first."

They lined up their shots, and Eric watched their movements. Zach was controlled where Caputo was loose, almost careless. Surprisingly, Caputo won the shoot-off. He glanced at Zach, but couldn't read if his friend cared or not.

Eric and Sam were next. While he'd never played pool with Zach or Caputo before, he and Sam had been meeting up on a monthly basis. As Sam counted down, he kept his eye on the far wall of the table. When it was time, he hit the ball precisely where he wanted to. Their balls ended up virtually tying, so Caputo ended up claiming the first shot and picked Eric for his team.

They had worked their way through about half the balls when Zach spoke up. "If you don't want things going sideways, you need to make things clear."

"I have made things clear."

Zach shook his head. "If things were clear, you wouldn't be having any communication issues. And the problem with communication is people bring their baggage into the conversation without the other person knowing about it."

Eric stared at him. "Baggage?"

"Yeah. You know some of her baggage, but you're never going to know all of it. Plus, she's going to have complicated feelings. You've got to lay yourself out on the line so she feels safe doing the same thing."

An itch formed between his shoulders. "Lay myself on the line?"

Caputo missed his shot, and Zach moved to the table to line up his. "Yeah. With the shit going on with her dad, she's probably feeling more than a bit vulnerable. Which means she's going to retreat to a safer place." He paused to hit the ball. And ended up sinking two thanks to a ricochet shot. He looked up at Eric. "Get inside her defenses before she completely blocks you out. Doesn't mean you have to do anything. But as long as she feels safe with you, you've got a chance."

They continued the game, and Sam and Zach ended up winning. Sam backed out of a second game, though. "I've got to head out. Surgery in the morning. Thanks for dinner and the game. Nice to meet you, Tony."

"Same."

After Sam left, Caputo began racking up the balls again. "Anyone up for Cut Throat? Winner buys a round for the whole bar?"

"I told Harry we wouldn't bet."

"It's not really betting. Plus, it's the winner who has to pay."

Zach shook his head. "Just roll with it, Eric."

"Fine. But if Harry kicks me out, I'm taking the two of you down with me."

Since Zach had won the previous game, he assigned the ball numbers for each of them to protect. He also took the break. Balls scattered all over the table, but the only one that fell in was one of Zach's.

Caputo was up next, and it turned out he was ruthless. Eric wondered if he actually made his money, at least partially, from being a pool shark. Before he lost his turn, he sank three more of Zach's balls and two of Eric's.

Eric focused on the play of the table. Zach's remaining ball was in a good position, but he'd have to kiss it to get the correct angle to push it into the hole. Caputo's balls were scattered all over the table. He'd probably do better to place the cue ball as far from his own balls as he could.

Instead, he went after Caputo's balls. He only sank one before he lost his turn.

Zach added another two of Caputo's balls to the count. They were down to five balls on the table. Caputo walked around the table before lining up his first shot. Zach's remaining ball went down. Then each of Eric's remaining balls in quick succession.

Eric shook his head and looked at Zach. "Where did you find this guy?"

Zach smiled a little. "Hollywood."

"They still have pool halls out there?"

"Of a sort."

Caputo grinned. "Don't worry. We can go another couple of rounds if you want a rematch."

"Go buy the round, Tony." Zach began pulling the balls out of the return and racking them again.

Eric looked around the bar. It had filled up with the evening crowd. Buying a round for everyone at Geraghty's would be a hell of a lot cheaper than buying a round for the house in Hollywood, but it wouldn't be cheap.

Caputo came back and placed the cue ball where he wanted it. "Good with the same numbers?"

"Yeah." Eric leaned against the wall and watched him. It felt like Caputo was shaking off another skin as he settled into the play. He became a bit more intense. More focused.

This time, it was Zach who won, but barely. Eric couldn't tell if Caputo had missed the shot that would have sunk Zach's last ball on purpose or not.

Zach said it was time for him to head out as well, as he had some kind of call he had to get on. Since he was Caputo's ride, they gathered up the equipment and returned it to Harry.

Caputo turned to him while Harry began cashing them out. "Zach's not wrong about being vulnerable to get your girl. Sometimes there are reasons you can't tell the whole truth, but you can still be honest about your emotions."

There was something there he was not quite catching, but before he could try to pin it down, Zach clapped him on the shoulder. "Figure out what you want to do, Eric. Libby seems like she'd be a good fit for you. You could do a hell of a lot worse."

Eric rolled his eyes. "Thanks for that."

Harry brought their checks back over. "Worse than what?"

Caputo jerked a thumb at Eric as he checked his bill. "Eric here is having lady troubles."

Harry grunted. "Figure out where the clit is, pay attention to it, and jerk yourself off afterwards if that's all she wants. Respect the lady."

The three of them stared at him.

"What? Read a romance book if you don't understand. How do you think I've kept my wife happy for almost twenty years?"

They each signed their checks and handed them back to Harry. When they were outside, they stood in the waning sunlight as it turned to evening, and looked at each other.

Caputo was the first one to speak. "Romance books?"

Zach finally shrugged. "Couldn't hurt."

Eric didn't think he'd pick up a romance, but since every single guy he'd talked to tonight said he'd have to open himself up to Libby emotionally, he'd have to figure out something.

And as he was driving back to his place, he realized the reason he felt so uncomfortable was because he'd never had a decent model of emotional vulnerability. But now he had Harry, of a sort. He didn't think he wanted marriage with Libby. Not right now. But he wanted something. A chance to find out if they wanted to explore something like marriage together.

But as he pulled into his driveway, he saw someone was sitting on his front steps.

Waiting for him.

And his gut sank when he recognized who it was.

His dad.

fifteen

LIBBY PULLED INTO MELODY'S DRIVEWAY. HER FRIEND'S TRUCK was parked up closer to the house, still dusty from the day as she'd spent it on-site at the Sullivan project. Mayzie looked over at her from the front seat and whined. The puppies yipped from the back.

She reached over and petted Mayzie on the head. "I know, but I'm possibly spending the night with Eric, and you can't be away from the puppies that long."

Mayzie looked into the back and let out a sigh. Libby laughed. "Come on. Let's get Melody, and you and the puppies can play in the back."

Mayzie followed her through the driver's side door, and up to Melody's front door. Libby rang the bell and then wondered if Melody might be in the shower. She waited a few minutes, and when Melody didn't answer, rang the bell again. She checked the car and saw three of the puppies had climbed up to the window and were watching them. Considering how big they'd gotten, she had the feeling that if the window was cracked more than the inch it was, they'd be wiggling their way out.

Melody opened the door just as Libby was contemplating the chaos of loose puppies. "Hey. Sorry about that. I had a call I needed to take."

Libby smiled. "No problem. Can you help me with the puppies? They're getting too big for me to handle by myself."

"Sure."

Libby opened the car door and did her best to make sure none of the puppies escaped. Melody caught Button right as she was about to tumble out of the car carrier.

Between them, they got the wriggling monsters transferred from the car to the house with no escapees. Melody had set up a little pen area in her living room, so Libby placed the puppies she carried into it.

Mayzie sniffed around the pen, and when she was satisfied, laid down next to it.

Melody put two of the puppies into the pen and then carried Button with her into the kitchen. "Want something to drink?"

Libby checked her phone. "Sure. I've got a little time before I'm supposed to meet Eric."

Melody brought two cans of alcohol spritzers back in with her. "I figured this was light enough since you're still driving tonight."

"Thanks." Libby cracked the can open and took a sip. It had a light raspberry-lemon flavor.

After putting Button into the pen to play with her siblings, Melody sat down on her couch. "Before you head over to Eric's, I need to tell you something."

Not liking the serious tone, Libby sat in the chair opposite her. Mayzie came over and laid her muzzle on Libby's knee. She took comfort in petting Mayzie's soft fur. "What?"

"I've been hearing people talk about the two of you

around town. Nothing malicious, but people are talking about how you're now a couple."

Libby sat back in the chair. It wasn't the worst news, like her father showing up in town demanding to have her taken into custody because of a court order.

"What exactly are they saying?"

"Just that you were spotted together at the fireworks show, cuddling."

Libby mulled that over as she took another sip of the spritzer. "That's not too bad."

"Like I said, nothing malicious. Honestly? People like you. Now they're just wondering if you're going to stick around."

Libby smiled. "Well, I did move into Andy Kavanaugh's rental."

Melody laughed. "There is that. How are the renovations going?"

"Fine." She looked at the puppies, who were tumbling over each other as they fought for control of a squeaky stuffed bee. "We stay out of the workers' way, and they leave us alone mostly. A couple will play with the puppies when we're outside and they're on break."

"Any takers yet?"

"So far, just you. No one else has mentioned anything to me about adopting. I think they're waiting for Sam to put them up on the adoption page."

"Just so everyone knows that Button will not be there."

Libby laughed. "I'm sure everyone in town is aware that you've already claimed Button."

Mayzie headed back to the pen and began nosing around the other side from the puppies. At one point, she crouched down and tried to slip her paw under the barrier. Libby saw another squeaker toy, this one in the shape of a penguin, just beyond her reach.

She got up and reached into the pen for the toy. The puppies saw what she was doing and raced to grab the penguin before she removed it. One of them even got their teeth on it, but with a light shake, Libby dislodged it. The puppy plopped onto its butt and whined for a moment before Button and the rest of the siblings tackled it.

Libby handed Mayzie the penguin, and she began chewing away on it. With the chorus of squeakers increasing in volume, she gave thanks that her phone showed it was time for her to head over to Eric's. "I need to go. Anything you need from me?"

"I'm good. Go have fun. Text me if you need me to keep them overnight."

Libby blushed, but nodded. "Thanks."

She headed out and was pulling into Eric's driveway less than five minutes later. She was halfway up the walk when he opened the door.

He smiled at her, and she smiled back. "Hey. Thanks for inviting me over."

"Sure." He pulled her into a hug and squeezed, but then released her and headed back to the kitchen.

Libby stood there for a moment. The hug was nice, but something felt off. She put her purse down next to the couch and followed him back.

There was a pot of water coming to a boil, and Eric was putting slices of fresh mozzarella on breaded chicken breasts. He opened the oven and placed the pan in.

"Chicken parmigiana?"

"Yep. I can't cook much, but I can do this."

"Did you make it from scratch?"

"Not really. I got the chicken breasts already prepared at the grocery store, and the sauce is from a can. But it's good and easy to throw together."

She noted his hair appeared to still be damp from the shower he likely took after getting home.

"Still, this is effort. Thank you for doing it."

He came back over and pressed a kiss to her forehead. "I'm happy to. Do you want something to drink?"

"Not at the moment, but I'd love wine with dinner if you have it."

"I picked up a cabernet at the store."

"That'll be perfect. Can I help with anything?"

He pointed at the fridge as he salted the water. "I've got a loaf of garlic bread in there. Can you put it on the rack below the pan in the oven?"

"Sure." The loaf was a large one, and, as she removed it from the wrapping, she inhaled the delicious scent of garlic and butter. "Did you also get this at the store?"

"Yep. I had to go in early this morning as they're usually sold out of it by lunchtime." Eric moved around the kitchen, cleaning up from the prep he'd already done. She admired the ease with which his body moved and looked forward to getting to explore it in bed later.

Fifteen minutes later, they were plating their dinners. The pasta had also been made fresh at the store, and Libby resolved to do some more exploring of the options the next time she was there.

Libby began heading to the front room, but Eric caught her elbow. "Out back. I've set up a table for us on my deck."

When he opened the back door for her, she almost stumbled in the doorway. He'd more than set it up. He'd turned it into a romantic little bistro. A trio of candles were flickering away on a small tablecloth-covered table.

"I hope you don't mind the scent of citronella because the bugs can get bad around here."

"I've noticed that."

He set his food down and then held her chair out for her. She smiled up at him. "Thank you. This is lovely."

He seemed to relax a bit. They spent dinner talking about what Eric's plans for the business were, and how Libby was doing with the work for her and Greer's business. Neither of them brought up her father, and Eric seemed to steer them back away from it anytime they came close.

She wanted to tell him about the call she'd had with Mr. Billings, but she also didn't want to ruin the mood. At one point, she reached out and put her hand on Eric's. He immediately turned his hand over and clasped his fingers around hers.

Feeling settled in a way she hadn't realized she needed, she focused back on her dinner.

When they were done, she offered to clean up.

He lifted her hand and kissed her palm. "I'll take the help. With two of us doing it, it'll go faster."

They brought their plates and silverware back inside. As she loaded the dishwasher, he began cleaning the pot and pan.

Every few steps, they'd brush up against each other. Finally, Libby slipped her arms around Eric from behind.

She felt his quick inhale as she began lifting his shirt up from his jeans. "Careful, I'm holding something breakable."

Libby smiled against his back. "I'm sure you can stand a little torture as you clean."

Eric rushed through what was left to be hand washed and then turned around in her arms. His hands, when they cupped her face, were still damp, but Libby forgot that as she sank into the kiss.

She pushed his shirt up as she wanted to feel all of his chest. Saturday night, she hadn't explored him, and she wanted that badly. He stripped his shirt off and tossed it...somewhere.

"Upstairs."

"Why?"

"Because that's where the condoms are."

"Oh. Good point."

He led her upstairs, their fingers entwined. Once they were in his bedroom, Libby jumped up, and he caught her. She cupped her hands around his face and kissed him. As they sank deeper into the kiss, his hands kneaded her ass. She rubbed up against his crotch, feeling his hardened cock.

All she could think of was getting it inside of her. She broke the kiss. "Bed. Now."

"Yeah."

He walked back until his legs hit the bed, and then he fell back. Libby screeched as she clung to him. Before she could say anything to him, he rolled them over and began undoing the shorts she was wearing. She lifted her hips so he could pull them down and off.

Eric paused over her, staring at her red lace panties. "You are gorgeous."

She shifted a bit as he placed one hand on her and began rubbing her skin. Her breath shuddered out of her as the roughness of the lace created an exquisite sensation. Eric moved and bent down to kiss her.

Libby wrapped her arms around him and held him tight. He slipped two fingers under the lace and began petting her clit. She moaned into his mouth, shifting her legs open further to encourage him.

He kissed his way down her neck until he met the collar of her shirt. "We should take this off."

"Yeah."

"And your bra."

"Do that."

His warm breath puffed against her skin as he laughed, raising goosebumps. "My fingers are busy." He stroked into her with one.

She lifted her hips. "They should get busier."

"You take off the shirt and bra."

He pushed up with his free hand and as he stroked in and out of her, his thumb circling her clit, Libby tried to focus on pulling off her top and remembering how her bra worked.

She eventually fumbled her way to being topless. The heated look in Eric's eyes was well worth the effort. "Now let's get rid of these panties."

As good as it felt to have some part of him inside her, she wanted to explore him. She gripped his wrist, and he stopped.

"What?"

"My turn."

"After I get you off."

She shook her head and pushed against his wrist. He didn't argue further, and pulled his fingers out of her. Then he did the hottest thing she'd ever seen, licking them clean.

"Eric..."

"You taste great, baby. You sure I can't taste more of you?"

She pushed against his shoulders. "I get to taste you first."

He groaned, but rolled onto his back. She undid his jeans, and was careful with his erection as it pressed so hard against the zipper, she could barely undo it.

As soon as she got his jeans and boxers down to mid-thigh, she paused and stared at his cock. He was thick through the shaft. Dark hair trailed down from his chest and formed a little nest for his balls. She reached out, wrapping her fingers around him. He hissed.

Libby grinned at him. "I promise to be gentle."

His voice, when he answered, was deep and gritty. "Don't be."

Taking him at his word, she squeezed him, bending her head to lick his tip. He groaned and threaded his fingers through her hair.

He smelled freshly showered but musky. She had experience giving guys head, but it had always felt like a chore before. With Eric, it was a gift of mutual pleasure.

He tapped her shoulder, and she lifted her head. "What?"

"Shift your ass up here."

Confused, she pulled back. "What?"

Eric curled up and grabbed her hips. "I want to eat you out while you blow me."

Caught by surprise, all she could do was let him manipulate her until her pussy was inches from his face, and she could feel his breath on her damp skin. "There we are."

He stroked through her folds with his tongue until he found her clit. Shivering, she bent back down and took his head into her mouth. The different angle took some getting used to, but she sank into the new experience.

Dimly, she heard him praising her and how she had the prettiest pussy. As he began sucking on her skin, she followed suit and worked more of him into her mouth. He grew even thicker in her hand.

Eric broke away from the attention he was giving her clit. "I'm going to come."

She appreciated the warning and kept going. Before, she'd always let her partners come on her chest, but she wanted to take Eric all the way.

He groaned and turned his head to lightly bite her inner thigh. She moaned around him at the contact, and that seemed to be all he needed as her tongue was soon coated.

Libby took her time licking him clean. He pushed his fingers into her and pumped steadily as he pressed against her clit. She soon was shaking as an orgasm ripped through her.

The sensation was too much, and she fell down with her face next to his softening cock.

She pressed a kiss against it.

A few minutes later, Eric began moving her again until she was face-to-face with him. He kissed her, and she felt his cock stirring against her hip.

She reached down and cupped him in her hand. That definitely induced even more hardening. "Where are the condoms?"

"Night stand." He pushed her down and settled between her thighs. His cock slid against her channel, and they both groaned at the contact. Eric shifted again as he reached out for his night stand. He pulled a couple of condoms out and then pushed up so that he was resting on his heels.

Libby pushed up onto her elbows so she could admire the man between her legs. From his work, he was nicely muscled, with some definition of his abs. Dark hair coated his chest, down to his cock. She watched as his fingers nimbly covered it with a condom. He crawled back over her, pressing his mouth against hers.

She relaxed back into the pillows and lifted her legs so they bracketed his hips. He reached between them and positioned his cock at her entrance. She reached down to stop him.

"What?"

"Lube."

"Shit. I'm sorry I forgot. Just a sec." He reached over again and pulled out the bottle. Coating the condom with it, he then poured a little down her center. He rubbed it around and into her. The feeling was intense after the orgasm, and she clenched down on his fingers.

"Fuck, Libby."

He shifted and pressed the head of his cock up against her and slowly pushed in. Her muscles relaxed, allowing the invasion.

When he was fully seated inside of her, he brushed her hair out of her face. "You good?"

The feeling of complete fullness had stripped her of the ability to speak. She could only nod and lift her hips. He slid the tiniest bit deeper and pressed against a magic spot.

He dropped his head into the crook of her neck and groaned. "I can't wait."

She hugged his hips with her thighs. "Don't."

He didn't. What followed wasn't pretty or elegant. It was a hard fuck that took them both under the waves of pleasure. When she began orgasming again, Libby didn't understand at first what was happening.

Eric pushed up, the look on his face feral. "Yes. Give it to me again." He began rubbing her clit as he pounded into her.

This time, the orgasm wiped her out as sensation exploded through her body. Eric shouted as his thrusts became erratic until he froze deep inside of her.

He then folded down, boneless, half-covering her. Her inner muscles continued to squeeze as aftershocks hit her. During one, Eric's hips jerked against her again. She bit her lip to keep from crying as the emotions overwhelmed her.

After a few minutes, Eric disengaged and went to the bathroom. He came back with a wet washcloth and cleaned her.

"I should go to the bathroom."

He nodded. "I'll be here."

She climbed over him, wanting to just cuddle for a few

minutes more, but the post-sex health gods called. Her legs were looser than the noodles they'd had for dinner, but she got to the bathroom and back.

Eric was exactly where she'd left him, but he'd pulled the blankets up. She crawled under them and rested her head against his shoulder.

As she let herself sink into sleep, she gave thanks for Eric's skills as a lover. But she also realized that great sex rarely solved the world's problems, and she had to talk to Eric about her father's latest plans. But that could wait until tomorrow.

sixteen

Eric parked his truck in Libby's driveway. She'd asked him to come with her to drop the puppies off at Sam's for the adoption process to begin. Melody was going to meet them there so she could claim Button.

He checked the back seat, making sure there wasn't anything there the puppies could chew on. It was going to be tight with all the puppies and Mayzie, but he was hoping he could convince Libby to go for a hike with him after.

Once he was satisfied there was nothing for the puppies to get into, he went and knocked on Libby's front door.

"Come in."

He opened the door, slowly at first, to make sure there were no little ones waiting for their chance to make an escape.

Libby was in the front room, all the puppies corralled in a playpen. She clasped her hand to her chest. "Thank goodness it's you. I still need to pack up their toys and food. Can you watch them? They keep trying to climb out of the pen, with a couple of them succeeding."

"Sure." Mayzie was lying on the couch, chewing on a bone as she watched her offspring. Libby had mentioned she'd weaned the puppies last week, and was not enthusiastic about them continuing to try to suckle.

Eric sat down next to Mayzie, who immediately rolled over and presented her belly for pets. He laughed. "You're only doing this because they're locked away, aren't you?"

She wriggled closer, and he took the hint to pet her.

Within a couple of minutes, he saw Libby's problem. Button and the next smallest of the siblings had figured out how to hook their baby claws into the mesh and climb up the pen's wall.

"Damn. Melody's going to have her hands full with you." Eric got up and lifted each puppy from the mesh and put them back down into the pen. He'd thought the little holes he'd spotted had come from them trying to chew their way out, but that obviously wasn't the case.

Libby came back into the room, carrying a large tote bag. Mayzie jumped down from the couch and went over to inspect the bag.

Eric stood up and held his hand out. "I'll take that out. Okay if it goes into the bed of the truck? I don't have much room otherwise."

"If you can secure it so it doesn't roll around, sure."

"Not a problem. Where's the thing you use for your backseat? I'll put it in, too."

She pointed to the space behind the front door, and he grabbed it on his way out.

Fifteen minutes later, they were on the road to Sam's. Mayzie was in the back with the puppies, but she'd put her snout on the console between the front seats. Eric glanced down at her. "Have you decided if you're keeping Mayzie?"

Libby nodded. "Yes. Everyone was right, and if I'm moving into a new phase of my life, I've got space for a dog." She reached down and rubbed Mayzie behind one of her ears.

When they arrived at Sam's, he pulled up close to the door so they could minimize the chances of a puppy getting away.

One of the nurses came out to help unload the puppies, and they were soon settled into an exam room. The puppies rooted around in the tote bag and pulled out a couple of the toys.

Sam came in just as Button yanked a bee squeaky toy from one of her siblings and began parading around the room with it. She immediately trotted over to him with her winnings and dropped it at his feet. He crouched down to rub her head and back. She immediately rolled over onto her back, and he laughed. "You're a very good dog, Button. Let's see how you and your siblings are doing."

He inspected each puppy, and they passed their exams with flying colors. He then checked Mayzie out, who sullenly allowed him to do what he needed to do. It was as he was helping her down onto the floor that Melody came into the room. Eric realized she was steaming, but as soon as she closed the door, she sat down on the floor, gathering all the puppies to her.

Sam looked at him, but he shrugged. Libby hurried over to her. Melody shook her head and wiped her eyes. She blew out a long breath, and when she spoke, her voice was raspy. "So, Sam. Can I take Button home with me?"

Sam didn't answer at first. Just went over to the counter where the most frequently used supplies were kept and grabbed a box of tissues. He held them out to Melody. Her laugh was watery, but she laughed. "Thanks. It's just allergies."

"Uh-huh. But in answer to your question, Button is in perfect health. You can take her home today after we process the paperwork. I also want you to schedule her next check up and round of vaccines."

"Sure."

Libby looked at Eric over her shoulder before she turned back to his sister. The concern he read in her face was the same he was feeling, but he knew she'd probably get a straight answer out of Melody faster than he would, so he shook his head at her.

Libby turned back to his sister. "Melody, do you want to talk?"

"No. I'm going to do the paperwork so I can take this sweet girl home, and I'll be fine. Promise."

Eric leaned against the exam table. "Need me to do anything?"

She shook her head. "Nope. Everything at the Sullivan site is under control, and so is Caputo."

Her voice hitched on the name, and Eric wondered if he needed to have words with Zach's friend. Before he could ask, Melody stood up. "I am fine. Seriously. Just let it be."

He realized that pushing any further would just piss her off. "Fine." He glanced at Libby. "I was going to suggest we head out for a hike with Mayzie, but if you want to go spend some time with Melody…"

Before he could finish, Melody cut in. "I told you I'm fine. Stop being my big brother. You two get on out of here. Please."

It was the please that did it. Sam let out a long sigh. "Give me a moment, and I'll get you set up so you can head home, Melody."

Twenty minutes later, Melody was on her way home with Button, and Sam's staff had processed the other puppies for adoption. The only thing left was to check out from Mayzie's exam. Sam stood next to them, making notes on Mayzie's chart while his office manager got them sorted. "I don't think we'll have any problem adopting them out.

Thanks to you walking them around town, they're pretty well known."

Libby reached down and petted Mayzie. "Thanks for roping me into caring for them. They helped distract me when I needed it."

Sam smiled at her. "Animals are the best. Sometimes better than humans."

Eric couldn't disagree with him. When his dad had shown up last week, it was to ask for a loan to get a guy off his back. His dad had never repaid a loan in his life, and Eric knew this would be the same.

He'd convinced his dad to go. Mainly with the threat that Uncle Stef should be back any day. Once his dad had gone, Eric had gone into the house and called the police department. Unsurprisingly, there were a few warrants out for his dad, so he gave them the head's up that he was in town. He wasn't sure if they'd picked him up or not, but if they did, he was probably safer in jail than out.

Calling the cops on his dad wasn't the best feeling, but he also needed to come to terms with the fact the old man would never be the father Eric wanted him to be. Hearing what Harry did to make sure his wife was happy earlier that night was the final nail in the coffin.

Mayzie nudged his thigh, breaking his reflective mood. "Ready for a walk?"

She barked, and Libby laughed. "Sure. Nothing too strenuous, though. I don't have water for her or hiking boots."

"Nothing strenuous, I promise."

The office manager handed Libby a packet of paperwork and a gift bag. "Welcome to dog mommyhood. I've got you scheduled for another checkup in two months."

Libby blinked. "Oh. Uh, thank you. Ummm...if I need to cancel?"

Eric wondered for a moment why she would need to cancel and then realized that she may be still considering going back to the city. A sour sensation began to bloom in his stomach.

"Just call at least twenty-four hours ahead of time."

"Great. Thanks." Libby glanced over at Sam, but he'd already focused his attention on his next patient.

"What did Bacon get into now?"

"The coffee grinds."

"Ralph, you need to throw those into your compost bin, not leave them out."

Eric swallowed a laugh and led Libby and Mayzie out to the truck. He opened the passenger doors for them, and Mayzie easily leaped up into the cab. Libby didn't leap, but she moved faster than he expected, denying him the opportunity of putting his hands on her curves.

He rubbed his hands on his jeans before closing the back passenger door and headed around to the driver's side. He started up the truck and pulled out.

Libby fiddled with the radio until she found a station she liked. "Do you mind?"

"Nope. Play whatever you want."

"Do you think Melody will be okay?"

He blew out a breath. "Yeah. She'll let me know if she needs something. And if she doesn't, I'll check in with Mom and Ana."

Libby chewed on her thumbnail. "I'm not sure about leaving the puppies there."

He reached over and gently pulled her hand from her mouth. Bringing it up to his mouth, he kissed her knuckles. "Do you doubt Sam and his staff will take good care of them?"

"No, but..."

"No buts. That staff has facilitated more adoptions than

you can count. They know exactly how to care for puppies just separated from their mama for the first time."

Her head fell back onto the headrest. "My head knows that, but my heart's hurting."

He kissed her hand again. "I'm sure it is. You and Mayzie did a great job with them. They're ready to go off to their new homes. I know this is bothering you, but what else? Did Mr. Billings call again?" The news she'd shared with him last week had been haunting him.

She shook her head. "I keep expecting something. I don't trust my father when he's quiet."

"Why?" Not that he didn't already have a horrible impression of her dad from what he was doing to gain control of her.

She was quiet as they entered the more heavily forested area of the county. The state park he was driving them to abutted his uncle's property. Libby rolled down her window and cooler air blew in.

Eventually, she shifted to face him. "When I was a little kid, one day I came home early from school because I was sick. My nanny had signed me out and picked me up. My father was home that day working on some project. My nanny and I were having lunch in the kitchen when he came out of his office for something. He hadn't expected me to be home, and he just froze when he saw me. He asked her what I was doing at home, and she explained how I was running a fever and had to come home." Libby went silent again and reached through the space between the seats to pet Mayzie.

"He didn't say anything to either of us after that. My nanny put me to sleep, and I somehow stayed asleep the entire night. When I woke up, it was to a different nanny in my room. When I called out, crying for the nanny I knew, my father came into my room and told me I was behaving like a child, and that my previous nanny was gone forever. I was to never mention her again."

"Jesus."

"Yeah. It's often harder to fight against my father than to just go along with whatever he wants you to do."

He reached over and squeezed her knee. "I'm sorry."

She shrugged. "When you grow up with something, it's your normal. Believe me, I know he's a shitty parent, and everything he did had nothing to do with me. But it's hard to break habits."

"You broke it when you opened your business with Greer. How did you do that?"

Libby laughed. "Greer's sheer force of will. And therapy. I'd started going to a therapist when I was in law school because even though I wanted to be there with my whole soul, I'd break out into hives anytime I was around the faculty. It was one of my professors who noticed me scratching my arms every class period who finally suggested I go see someone. He was familiar with my father."

"It sounds like quite a few people are familiar with your father."

She shrugged again. "It's hard not to be when you practice law in this state or run in certain social circles. Did I ever tell you that Mrs. Smith has met him?"

"No."

"She doesn't have a good impression of him. But then, no one who's met him seems to like him. A lot respect him, though, because of the power he's accumulated."

"And now you're fighting him in court." Eric spotted the entrance to the state park ahead and slowed to make his turn.

"All thanks to Mr. Billings. I honestly don't know that if

I had anyone else as my lawyer that I'd be able to fight him."

"I'm glad you found someone to fight for you."

"So am I."

Eric drove to the second parking lot, which was closer to the walking loop that ran around one of the small lakes in the area. When they arrived, the lot was empty.

They climbed out, and Eric led the way to the trailhead. "When you're done with this case, what do you think you'll do?"

Libby looked at him. "I don't know when the case will be over with. My father can be tenacious when he's not getting his way, so he could drag this out. It would have to take something major for the court to dismiss the case with prejudice in my favor. Even then, I'm sure he'd come up with something else to harass me with."

Eric reached out and took hold of her hand. "Okay, in a perfect world, what would you want to do?"

She squeezed his hand. "I'm not sure. I don't feel like I can give myself permission to dream just yet."

He lifted their hands and kissed her knuckles. "Dreaming about the future can help you carry on through the rough times."

"But what if you're in the habit of not dreaming?"

He thought that over for a moment. "You said you'd gone to therapy. What would your therapist say to that?"

Libby leaned her head against his shoulder. "You probably should be a therapist."

Eric gave an exaggerated shudder. "And listen to everyone's problems? If I'd wanted to do that, I would have become a bartender. Better tips." He grinned when she laughed. He tugged her hand. "Come on, let me show you something."

She looked up and waggled her brows. "Is it something dirty?"

He brushed a kiss against her forehead. "Get your mind out of the gutter. I don't want to traumatize Mayzie. No. There's an overlook if we break away on this side trail."

They hiked up to the overlook and sat down on a bench that had been constructed just off the path. Eric put his arm around Libby's shoulders, tucking her into his side. "Okay, I want you to pretend that the case with your dad has been settled in your favor. And he's not started any other lawsuits. What do you want the next six months to look like?"

Libby lifted her head and kissed his jaw. It took everything in him to not tilt his head and meet her kiss. He needed her answer to his question. She must have realized she couldn't distract him from his goal, and sighed.

"I don't think I want contact with him again, but he's my father."

He brushed his hand up and down her upper arm. "I get it. But you have a choice. Again, think about what your therapist would tell you to do."

She dug her knuckles into his side. "You've never been to a therapist, have you?"

"Not really. Tried a few, but none of them seemed like they knew anything."

Libby leaned into him and hugged him. "It's hard. You have to be vulnerable. If you're not willing to be vulnerable, it won't work. And a good therapist doesn't tell you what to do. They'll advise you on how to use tools, but it's on you to determine what path you want to take."

Eric chewed on her words. "You're telling me I should try again?"

"Nope. Just telling you why your past attempts might

not have worked out. It's up to you if you want to try again."

They were silent for a few minutes, but to Eric, it was a peaceful silence. They were together, even if they were lost in their own thoughts. In the distance, he saw a bald eagle swoop down and pick up a fish from the lake.

He squeezed Libby's shoulders. "Getting back to your dreams. What do you want to happen?"

Libby settled even deeper into his embrace, but didn't say anything. Mayzie started exploring as far as her leash would allow. He turned his head and pressed a kiss against the top of Libby's head. Maybe he should back off, but he felt that this was important. He needed to know if she saw him in her future. Because, he realized, he saw her in his.

Not the most comfortable of realizations, but he wanted to come home at night and hear about her day of dealing with thorny contracts and finding out what Mayzie had discovered on her walks.

Taking them to some of his favorite places in the area. Going to the beach on days off. Maybe even taking a trip up to Canada and checking out Toronto or Montreal. Family dinners with his mom and Melody.

His phone rang.

Knowing that coverage could be spotty here, he tugged it out of his pocket as fast as he could.

Uncle Stef's name showed as the contact. He hadn't been expecting Uncle Stef back in town for another week, but knew if he was calling, it was important.

He answered the call. "Hey, Uncle Stef. What's up?"

Libby pushed up and looked at him. He released his hold on her and held his finger up to his lips.

"Where are you?"

"At the state park. Where are you at?"

"At my house with Melody. She said I had a visitor. Is she with you?"

Eric frowned at the tone he heard in his uncle's voice. "Yeah."

"Good. Come on back. I need to talk to her, and this isn't a conversation I want to be having on the phone."

"Okay."

Before he could say anything else, Uncle Stef cut in. "See you in half an hour." And hung up.

Eric shook his head. "I'm sorry. Uncle Stef wants to talk to you now. Are you up to it?"

Libby closed her eyes and breathed in and out deeply a few times. "I think so? I mean, I want to know what he knows about my mom."

"We should head back, then. You probably heard he's expecting us in half an hour."

They headed down the path back to the truck, and it was Libby who reached out and held his hand. "Is he always so brusque?"

"Yeah. Uncle Stef always said he didn't believe in talking more than he needed to."

Libby was rubbing the back of his hand with her thumb, and he realized she was nervous. He stopped them in the middle of the trail and kissed her.

Only when they were each out of breath did he come up for air. "It'll be okay, Libby. I promise. Uncle Stef's brusque, but he'd never hurt you."

She closed her eyes and nodded. "I believe you. It's just, I never thought I'd ever hear any stories about my mom. No one talks about her. Ever. And I don't have any family on that side."

Eric wondered if that was the truth. From everything he observed, he could totally believe her father lying about her not having family on her mom's side. It would be absolutely evil if that was the case, but not completely out of the realm of possibility.

He pulled her in tight for a hug. "Come on. Let's get some answers from Uncle Stef."

As they walked back to the truck, he just hoped the answers his uncle may have would help Libby, and not tear her away from him and Sunflower Falls.

seventeen

LIBBY CLIMBED OUT OF ERIC'S TRUCK. IN THE TIME SHE'D BEEN IN Sunflower Falls, she hadn't come back to Stef's home. The bushes were a bit more trimmed, and she'd bet it had been Eric who'd taken care of that. If there was only one thing she'd learned about Eric Keller, it was that he was loyal and took care of the people in his small circle. She thought she'd learned a lot more about him, but the care he gave his people was a bright light.

The door opened, and it was Melody standing there with Button in her arms. Libby opened the back door so Mayzie could jump out. Melody smiled at them and looked a bit more relaxed.

Eric gave Button a scratch behind her ears, which turned her into a wriggling mass of fur. "When did you get here?"

"I drove by on the way home from Sam's and spotted Stef's car in the driveway."

Eric looked at her, ignoring Button, who was trying to gnaw on his fingers. "Are you okay?"

"I am. Really. How was the hike?"

Eric glanced at Libby. "Okay."

She knew he was thinking about how she'd never answered him. She still didn't know how to answer him. The thought of her father out of her life was a gaping black hole. Not that it would be a loss. It was just a thought she had never once entertained. She couldn't imagine him not in her life.

Even this last month that she'd been here, he'd always been in the background. Until he died, she knew he would always try to force some presence into her life.

"Come on in. Uncle Stef's up in his attic. He said he had to find something."

The inside of Stef Keller's home was spare, to put it kindly. He had a couch that looked older than Libby from the fabric choice. The TV was a flatscreen, but it was small. There weren't even any decorations on the walls. He had a fireplace with a mantel, and that housed four photos. One of Eric, Melody, and Nina Keller next to a Christmas tree. Two looked like they were Eric's and Melody's high school graduation portraits. And the last one was a group of people outside an elegant house. She wondered if it was the crew from the renovation show.

Footsteps on the stairs filled the space.

Stef Keller walked through the doorway into the living room. "Did I hear the door open, Mel?" He was rooting around in a box.

"Hey, Uncle Stef."

Stef Keller looked up, and she could immediately see the family resemblance between him and Eric. Stef had the same sharp bone structure and blue eyes, but his hair had faded to a salt-and-pepper look with his dark brown hair.

Stef met her gaze. "Liberty?"

She smiled at him. "Libby, please. Very few people I consider friends call me Liberty."

He nodded. "Nice to meet you." His voice cracked on the

last word, and he cleared his throat. "I'm sorry to have written you out of the blue like that. I'm sure it was a shock."

Libby glanced over at Eric, but he shrugged. She knew if she looked at Melody, she'd get the same response. When she turned back to Stef, he had a sad, but compassionate, expression on his face. "A bit of one, but I'm very glad you did. I'd like to learn more about my mother, if you'd be willing to share. I never knew her."

He sighed. "I didn't know that she'd died until years after she did. I just want you to know that, and I'm sorry."

"Thank you. Can we sit down?"

"Oh. Yeah. Sure."

She followed him over to the couch. "Is it okay if I let my dog off her leash?"

He glanced over at Melody, who'd sat on the floor to play with Button. "I'm not sure with the puppy."

Eric looked at Melody. "You didn't tell him?"

Stef frowned and looked between the two of them. "Tell me what?"

Melody rolled her eyes. "Mayzie is Button's mom. They're fine."

"Oh. I guess that's okay, then."

Libby unhooked Mayzie's leash, but she stayed close to Libby and laid down at her feet. She smiled at Stef. "She just weaned all the puppies last week, so she's been a little leery of letting them get close."

Stef laughed. "I'd bet." Then he cleared his throat. "I should probably be upfront about this. Your mom and I were more than friends."

Libby blinked. "Oh. Okay." She wasn't sure what to do with that information. It didn't surprise her that her mom had been involved with men other than her father, but why would her mom have chosen her father? She'd sometimes wondered if he'd changed after her mom's death, but anyone she'd met who knew them while married said her father always had a stick up his ass.

He pulled a photo out of the box and handed it to her. It was a photo of a much younger Stef and her mother standing in a kitchen. He had his arms around her, and they were both grinning at the camera. There was a ring on her finger. Libby traced it. "Were you engaged?"

Stef cleared his throat. "No. When I met her, she said she wore the ring to remind her why she never wanted to go back. She never took it off."

Libby looked up at him. "What?"

He rubbed his face. "I'm not proud of it, but I knew she was engaged to someone else. At least, I knew she had been. I was on a job in the early years of the show, and she worked at a restaurant we went to regularly. We started talking, and one thing led to another."

"Where?"

"Near Pittsburgh."

"Pittsburgh?"

"Yeah. She mentioned she used to live in New York, but she'd left her fiancè, and didn't think he'd find her in Pittsburgh."

"She didn't think he'd find her? Was she worried about him?"

Stef's jaw worked. "Yeah. After a couple of months, she seemed to relax a bit. We started going out more and more rather than just meeting up at the restaurant and going to her place or mine."

Dread curdled in Libby's gut. Mayzie must have picked up on something as she got up, put her chin on Libby's thigh, and whined. Libby ran her hand over Mayzie's head, trying comfort her pet. And maybe herself. Her voice was quiet when she finally found words. "What happened?"

Stef seemed to collapse a bit in on himself. "I'm not sure. I went to pick her up after we finished filming one day. She was on the afternoon shift, so the plan was I'd have dinner at the restaurant's bar and hang out like usual. Then we were going to head to a late movie.

"When I got to the restaurant, the manager came over to me immediately. She knew we were dating. Apparently, some guy in a suit came in and demanded to speak with your mom. No one recognized him, but as soon as she saw him, she dropped the tray of drinks she was carrying. The manager let them have her office for a talk, but she couldn't hear much of what they were saying with the door closed."

Stef rubbed his face again before continuing on. "Turns out it was your dad. To this day, I don't know how he convinced her to go back to New York and marry him. But he did. She quit as soon as she walked out of that office. The manager said she didn't look well and offered to help, but your mom told her it was fine."

He looked at Libby, rubbing his palms against his knees. "Believe me, if I'd know where he'd taken her, I would have gone after them. She didn't talk much about him, but she'd made it clear she was done with him."

"I believe you."

Stef dug around in the box again and pulled out a post-card featuring Times Square. He handed it to her. Libby flipped it over and just saw the words, "I'm sorry. Monica." She'd addressed it to Stef in care of a production company. "When did you get this?"

"About a year later. I put it away. It was clear she wouldn't be coming back. But then, about fifteen years ago, I went through a bad breakup. I thought I'd see if she'd left your dad, and did an internet search. I found her obituary."

Libby reached out and put her hand over Stef's. He turned it over and squeezed. "I'm really sorry, Libby." He took another deep breath. "Since she was gone, I thought I'd check up on you. It was just a few times since I found out she had died. The last time, I came across your engagement announcement. Thought it was a sign and wrote you."

"Thank you, Stef." Libby swallowed back tears. She didn't know what to say beyond that. Wishing her mother stayed with Stef would mean wishing away her own existence. But she also didn't know if it was right for her mother to return to her father. The few pictures she had seen, her mother looked...resigned. She looked down again at the photo of her mother and Stef. Happiness radiated from both of them.

Mayzie licked her wrist. Libby laughed, but even she heard the tears in it. "I appreciate you writing, Stef. I don't know that I'd be here without your letter."

She definitely wouldn't have fled her own proposed wedding without it. And knowing that she'd taken steps to claim her own independence gave her strength.

Libby looked up at Eric. She saw the caring and the understanding in his expression. She handed the postcard back to Stef. "Thank you. Thank you for loving my mother, and for reaching out to me."

"She was a good woman." He carefully put the postcard back into the box.

Before she handed the photo back, she traced her mother's face. "Can you make a copy of this for me? Please?"

He nodded and cleared his throat. "Sure. I've got a few others you might like."

"I would." She handed the photo back to him. Cleared the tears from her eyes. She had work to do. "Eric, can you drive me back to my place?"

"Sure."

She hooked Mayzie's leash back to her harness. "Come on, Mayzie."

Neither Melody nor Stef said anything further to her. She wasn't sure why, but she appreciated the silence as she wrestled with her thoughts.

It was clear from Stef's story that her father wouldn't just let her go. She'd known that in her mind when he'd filed the case to have her placed under guardianship, but hearing the story about her mother settled the knowledge into her bones.

Why her father was the way he was didn't matter at this point. He'd proven his character over and over again while she'd been growing up. He'd never allowed anyone to check him.

She didn't care. She was her own person, and she'd make sure he could never interfere with her life again.

Eric climbed into the driver's seat. "You okay?"

She looked over at him. "I will be."

He pulled out of the driveway and headed toward her house. She'd have to let Andy know that she'd be away for an unknown amount of time. And arrange with him to have her things packed up if she wasn't able to come back before the end of her lease.

Her brain was so busy creating all the lists of what she needed to do that she didn't realize they were back at her house until Eric took her hand and squeezed. She snapped out of it. "Sorry. I've got a lot to do."

"About what?"

"Taking my father down."

Eric stared at her. "Okay. He absolutely deserves to be knocked out of your life. Are you going to call Mr. Billings with this info?"

"No. I need to go back to the city."

He blinked. "What?"

"I need to go back. He's not allowed to get away with this anymore, Eric. First, he ruined my mom's life. She was happy, Eric. So happy." Tears began running down her face, but she couldn't bring herself to wipe them away. "He ruined that. He ruined her. Then, when she died, he tried to wipe her out of my existence. He never refers to her. I've only seen her picture a few times in my life because he never kept any. Anytime someone gave me a photo of her, he got rid of it. Said I didn't need any reminders of the past. Now he's trying to have me put away. No. He doesn't get to ruin my life like he ruined hers."

Eric reached up and wiped away the tears on her cheek with her thumb. "But you're not safe back there. Greer said."

"Fine. I'll call her and let her know I'm coming."

"I'll go with you."

Libby immediately shook her head. "No. This is my fight."

"What do you mean, this is your fight? Libby, I care about you. You should not have to face your dad on your own."

Her lips twisted as she reached up to cup his face. "That's what you're not getting, Eric. I'm not facing him on my own. I'll have Greer and, more importantly, Mr. Billings in my corner. My father doesn't know who you are, and I'd like to keep it that way."

"Libby..."

"No, Eric. You don't need to rescue me. I can handle this on my own. I have to handle this on my own. My father is never going to respect me. I know that, but I need to be able to respect myself. And that means facing him down."

He closed his eyes, and Libby knew this was taking a toll on him. If she could have avoided this, she would have, but running out of town without telling him would have been even worse.

"Are you going to come back?"

She let out a long breath. "Is it enough to say that I'd like to?"

"No."

She bit her lip to hold in a sob. "At least you're being honest."

"Libby, please…"

She pressed her fingers against his lips. "Eric. Please. Not fighting me anymore is how you can support me. Can you do that for me?"

He was quiet, but held her fingers to his lips and kissed them. "Yeah. At least keep me updated, will you?"

"I can promise you that if I can't keep you updated, Greer will."

"Fine. I'll have to live with that."

He carried what remained of the puppy transfer into her house and looked around. "I can stop by periodically and make sure everything's fine."

Knowing that he needed to have something to do for her, even if it was something easily done by another person, she nodded. "Thank you. That would be great. I'm going to let Andy know I'll be gone for a bit."

"How long?"

She went over and hugged him. "I don't know. However long it takes to get my father out of my life."

He stood there for a minute and then wrapped his arms around her. Squeezed her so tightly that she could hardly draw in a breath. "Be safe for me. Come back."

"I'll do my best."

He cupped her chin with one hand and raised it to give her a kiss. It went from one of comfort to searing heat in moments. "Got to have you. One last time."

"Upstairs."

He picked her up and carried her up the stairs to her bedroom. Without words, they stripped each other, baring all. Libby felt as if layers of skin had gone with her clothes.

Eric laid her down on the bed, kissing her while he began petting her core. She shifted her legs, giving him entrance. He stroked in a couple of times before pushing up and reaching for the bedside table.

He pulled out the lube she'd begun keeping there and squirted some where his hand had been.

She arched up as he stroked in again. "Yes."

"I'm going to make sure you never forget me."

"Do it."

He kept his gaze on her while he worked her over. When she finally orgasmed, he reached for the table again for a condom and had it on in seconds. He shifted, positioned himself, and pressed into her.

Libby lifted her legs, wrapping them around his hips. He shifted again, entwining his fingers with hers as he pressed her hands into the bed.

She squeezed him with her inner muscles, needing to claim him as much as he was claiming her. Imprint on him. Make him always remember the feel of her body.

Remember the feel of his.

"Oh, Libby." He bent down and began kissing away her tears.

She couldn't help them. Breaking the hold of his hands, she reached up and pulled his body close against hers.

That was how each of them came, wrapped around each other so tight that neither air nor light could come between them.

When it was over, Eric pressed his forehead to hers. "Come back."

"I'll try."

eighteen

Eric wiped the sweat from his forehead. He and Uncle Stef were almost done with the finish carpentry in the kitchen. The cabinets gleamed a rich golden tone highlighting the ripples in the curly maple.

Nora Sullivan had provided a generous budget, and her mom had taken her up on it for the kitchen. In fact, Nora was going to do a walk-through tomorrow with her parents to check on the status, and he wanted at least the kitchen complete. They were still weeks away from finishing the house, but they were finally at the point where the client could see the decisions all coming together. The backsplash was an interesting cut river rock tile, and the countertops were a dark blue-grey soapstone.

This kitchen would see a lot of action as Mr. and Mrs. Sullivan hosted family get togethers. His mom had already received a housewarming invitation from Mrs. Sullivan.

And if there was one thing Eric hated doing, it was disappointing his mom.

"You done with that strip yet?" Uncle Stef stood nearby, chugging down an energy drink.

Eric positioned the nail gun and fired in the last nail along the footing of the island. "All done. How about you?"

"All set here. Ready to clock out?"

"Almost. I need to check with the rest of the crew first."

Stef replaced the cap on his bottle. "Let's get going then. Want to grab a burger at Geraghty's with me?"

Eric smiled. It had been a while since he and Stef had gone to Geraghty's. When he'd been a teen, Stef would take him there for some one-on-one time whenever he wasn't away shooting the current season of the show. It had been a needed respite, especially after his dad left town the last time.

"Yeah, that'd be good. Give me about fifteen."

"Fine. I'll check to see what's on the punch list in the bathroom, so I know what to bring tomorrow."

Eric headed up to the second floor, where his crew had settled in for the day. They'd installed and mudded almost all the drywall. He found Donna standing in the master bathroom for this floor, measuring out where they would be installing the cabinetry and fixtures later that week.

"Everything good up here?"

She looked over her shoulder. "Everything's good in here. All the measurements are still solid."

When she didn't continue, he frowned. Her tone indicated there was something off. "What's wrong?"

Donna rubbed her forehead. "My kid texted me about an hour ago. They were on social media and caught that there's something going on with Libby's case."

Eric grimaced. Libby's case had turned into a media circus over the last couple weeks when her lawyer accused her father—in open court—of hiding, and possibly embezzling, trust assets that Libby should have had access to.

Her father had a large enough reputation in the state and, apparently, across the nation, that questions were now being raised about his business dealings. Social media had gotten wind of it thanks to the case's resemblance to a few other high profile legal cases, and the fact that Libby looked good on camera.

Not that she was talking. Libby never talked to the press. They'd only taken photos when she'd been walking into the courthouse, or out walking Mayzie. Because of all the press attention, Zach had arranged a bodyguard for her.

Eric hadn't been happy about the speculation he'd seen in a couple places about Libby's torrid romance with said bodyguard, but the one time they talked about it, she laughed.

Libby had assured him the bodyguard had been informed of her relationship with Eric. "Besides, I think Michael's got a broken heart from a past relationship. The only baggage I want to deal with is yours." It had been a month since they'd had that conversation.

When Donna tugged on her ear, he focused back on her. Ear-tugging Donna never meant anything good. "What's the latest?"

"Apparently, there's been a special closed courtroom session called by the judge. Everyone's speculating about what that means for the case."

"When is it supposed to be?"

"Tomorrow morning at nine."

Eric pulled his phone out of his pocket, even though he knew there weren't any messages waiting for him. He still checked both his texting app and email. But there was nothing from either Libby or Greer. Libby had gone radio silent over the last week, and Greer hadn't gotten back to him after the last text he'd sent a couple days ago asking for an update.

Last night, he'd messaged Melody, who said she also

had nothing from either of them. He looked at Donna. "Thanks."

Donna nodded. "We should be able to do the last of the prep work on this tomorrow. Plumber is scheduled for the day after to rough everything in, and then installation of the fixtures and cabinetry on Monday."

"Okay. Tell everyone good work for me."

She saluted. "Will do."

He headed back downstairs. Stef was out front talking with some of the crew. For now, he had the first floor to himself. He would have preferred to make the call from behind a door, but there weren't any to be had on this level.

Pulling up the office number for B&H, he selected it. It rang several times before switching over to voicemail. All he got was Greer's voice instructing him to leave a message and someone would call him back when available.

Eric growled, but waited until he heard the tone. "Greer, call me back when you get this. I know you're checking it every day. I heard some news."

He hoped that would be a vague enough message to get her worried enough about what he'd heard and return his call.

Blowing out a breath, he shoved his phone back into his pocket. Since her return to the city, he and Libby hadn't talked nearly enough. He had never imagined how much he'd miss having her in his life. He'd gotten so used to having her around that he still turned to comment on something or get her opinion.

He even missed Mayzie. Not that he was alone in that. There were kids in town who'd stopped to ask him when Mayzie was coming back. Not even the fact that Button and the other puppies were still in town made a difference.

There was a knock on a window, and he looked up to

see Stef peering inside. His uncle held up his hands and pointed to his watch.

"I'm coming." He did a quick check, putting away a couple of tools that hadn't made their way back into the case. He and Stef had done good work today. The kitchen and most of the main floor were ready. Tomorrow, after the tour with the Sullivans, they'd install the bookcases that had been ordered, and do any remaining finishing work before helping to work on closing out the second floor.

When he got outside, he wiped his hand across his face. The breeze from the lake helped cool down the heat of August, but they still had weeks of summer left.

"You finally ready?" Stef came over and hooked his thumbs in his jeans pockets.

"Yeah..." His phone buzzed with an incoming text. He pulled it out, read the message, and swore.

"What's wrong?"

Eric rubbed his jaw, trying to relax it. "Not here. Mind if I catch a ride to Geraghty's with you?"

"Sure. Drop you back here after?"

"Yeah."

Stef waited until they'd pulled away from the site. "What happened?"

"There's apparently a special closed door court session happening tomorrow on Libby's case, and I called Greer for an update. She texted me she'd call me when she could."

"Greer?"

"Libby's business partner and best friend. The only communication I've been able to have with her in the last week has been through email, and that was all business. She's avoiding me."

"Libby or Greer?"

"Both of them. Libby hasn't returned any of my calls, texts, or emails."

Stef hummed, but said nothing for a few minutes. His uncle had usually just sat in silence until Eric came to his own conclusions about whatever was bothering him. And then told Eric he was on the right track or way off base.

This time, Eric shifted in his seat and stared at Stef until his uncle glanced in his direction. "Well?"

"Well? You're the one who deals with them. I'm not about to tell you what might be happening."

"Should I go down to the city or not?"

Stef rubbed the back of his neck. "Would it help or hurt her case if you were to suddenly show up?"

Eric looked out to watch the edges of Sunflower Falls thin out. "I don't know. When she first left, she told me she didn't want her dad to know about me."

"Why?"

He shrugged. "Don't know exactly. But he's obviously vindictive."

Stef tapped his thumb against the wheel. "He never came after me."

Eric looked back at him. "Did he know about you?"

"Doubt it. I had no idea where they lived, so I never got in touch with Monica. And, like I told Libby, the only contact I had from her after she left was that postcard that got sent to the production offices."

Eric spent the rest of the ride to Geraghty's chewing that over. The times he and Libby had talked since she'd gone back, they'd focused on what was going on in Sunflower Falls, and what the people Libby had met were doing. She'd told him she wanted him to be a break from the case, so they never talked about her father, either.

Stef pulled into the parking lot, and they got out. This time there was no fortuitous meeting with Sam, or Zach and Caputo, for that matter. A few other locals had installed themselves at the bar, so Stef headed back to the empty seats past the pool tables.

Harry was manning the bar and service again tonight, so he came over with a handful of napkins and wrapped utensils. "What do you want?"

They ordered burgers, appetizers, and drinks, and Harry headed back to the bar to put the order in.

Eric stared at him for a bit before turning to Stef. "I was in here a couple of months ago with Sam and Zach."

"Yeah?"

"Yeah. When we were leaving, Harry told us the secret to keeping a woman happy was to know where the clit is and read romance novels."

Stef choked on a laugh. When he finally got himself under control, he shook his head. "He's probably not wrong. He and Jolene have never had a fight, to the best of my knowledge. Since the day they met, they've been attached at the hip."

Harry came back with their pints. "What's wrong with you?"

Stef waved and took a sip of his beer. Harry scowled and looked at Eric. "I don't want to call an ambulance for him."

Eric grinned. "He'll be fine. I told him your secret to keep a woman happy."

"Clit and romance. Works every time."

Stef snorted into his beer as Harry headed back to the bar. Eric slid down into his seat and shook his head. "Probably best not to drink around him when he's about to say something."

"Probably."

They sat in comfortable silence, drinking their beer and then eating the onion rings delivered hot from the kitchen.

Stef picked up the last one. "When are you thinking about going to the city?"

Eric rubbed his hand against his knee. "Should I? I mean. I really want to, but I also don't want to cause trouble for Libby. And I'm sure I wouldn't be able to get into the courtroom tomorrow morning, even if I could get there in time."

Stef didn't immediately answer, but pulled out his phone. After tapping away at it, he put it face up on the table and slid it over to Eric.

He frowned down at it, but picked it up. At first, he didn't understand what he was seeing. Then he did. "Fuck."

"I saw that when I was waiting for you outside." On Stef's phone was a news alert about Libby's case—calling her the Scammed Little Heiress—with a photo of her face buried in Mayzie's neck. "I was going to tell you about it, and then you looked like your bike had gotten run over again."

"I loved that bike."

"Bet you love Libby even more."

Eric rubbed his face with both hands. "I haven't told her. I knew things were getting intense before she left, but I didn't realize how much I was going to miss her when she did."

"It rips your guts out. Especially if she never comes back. The pain'll heal, but you're never going to be the same again."

Eric stared at his uncle. "Think she's never coming back?"

Stef shrugged. "She seemed nice enough, but she might feel like she's better off in the city for whatever reason."

"I don't know if I can move there."

"Who said you had to move there?"

"If that's where she wants to live, I need to figure it out."

Stef finished what remained in his pint and signaled

Harry to bring him another one. "Listen, if living in the city is going to be what's best for her, and you want to be with her, then, yeah. You need to figure it out. But don't go making assumptions about what she wants to do. If there's one thing I've learned in my life when it comes to relationships, it's that you have to have honest conversations with whoever you're with. And sometimes you think you're having an honest conversation with them, and they're hearing something completely different."

Harry came over and placed a pint down in front of both of them. He crossed his arms against his chest. "He's right. Jolene and I can't talk mind to mind, so we've had to learn. Go watch some YouTube. Burgers should be out in a couple of minutes."

Stef rubbed his hand over his mouth as Harry walked away. "Again, he's not wrong. Figure out how you two best communicate and practice."

Eric scowled at him. "It'd help if I could actually talk with her."

Stef picked up his beer. "Then maybe it is time for you to head to the city. It's not like you have to walk into court with her for everyone to see, but you can let her know that you're there and you want to see her."

"Would you mind handling things over at the Sullivan site for me? Melody's up to her eyeballs with stuff she has to handle over at Caputo's." Eric spotted their food coming out of the kitchen.

Stef nodded. "Sure."

They spent the next fifteen minutes just focused on their burgers and fries. Harry always made sure the kitchen staff knew they were the most important part of the crew, and it showed. The food had never wavered in quality.

Eric picked up some fries. "Uncle Stef?"

"Yeah?"

"Do you ever regret not being able to make something with Libby's mom?"

Stef paused in the middle of lifting the last of his burger to his mouth. He then set it back down. "That's a heavy question."

"I'm sorry. Forget it."

Stef waved his hand. "No. It's heavy, but it's a good one to ask." He blew out a breath. "Yeah. I do. Don't know if it would have changed Monica dying from cancer. I may have lost her, no matter what. And it would also mean that Libby wouldn't be here. So, seeing you happy with Libby? No. I don't regret not being able to make something with Monica. I'm just sorry that she endured whatever she did before she died, and that she didn't get to see the kind of person her daughter grew up to be."

Eric smiled at him. "You're a generous man."

"No. I'm not. I'm hoping her father has his entire business dismantled, and gets put away for the rest of his life. It sounds like he's an abusive asshole who deserves to be taken out back and taught the proper way to treat people."

The reminder of what Libby was dealing with had Eric scowling again. "I need to get in contact with her or Greer and let them know I'm coming."

Stef picked up his beer and drained the rest of it. "You'll figure it out. Let's get you back to your truck so you can pack and get to bed."

Twenty minutes later, Stef pulled in behind Eric's truck at the Sullivans'. He looked over at his uncle. "Thanks, Uncle Stef."

Stef clapped him on the back. "Listen. Things weren't right enough for me to make a go of it with Monica. Go let Libby know you love her and then do whatever you need to do to support her. And then get both your asses back here. You may think New York's the best place for her, but from everything I've heard, she did a damn good job of settling in right here in Sunflower Falls. She can always head into the city when she needs to."

Eric laughed. "Thanks again." He climbed out of the truck and watched as Stef pulled away. His uncle had never been one to mince words. He thought Eric had a chance with Libby, so he'd better believe what Stef said.

He thought about calling Melody to let her know what was going on, but decided to swing by her house instead. When he got there, all the lights in the house were on. He frowned, but didn't hear any music or loud voices indicating she had anyone over.

He knocked on her door, and when she didn't answer, rang her bell. He was about to push it again when her door swung open. She stood there in a robe, hair mussed and face flushed.

"Shit. Am I interrupting something?" He hadn't seen another car, and did not want to let his mind go down alternative paths.

"No. No. Uh...nap. I fell asleep on the couch after I got home."

There was no way he was going to challenge that obvious lie. "I just wanted to tell you I'm heading down to the city tomorrow. I need to talk to Libby."

Melody frowned. "Talk to Libby? What do you mean? Haven't you been talking with her?"

"She hasn't taken my calls in over a week, and she hasn't returned any of my emails. Neither has Greer."

His sister crossed her arms over her chest and began tapping her foot. "Why are you going down there, then?"

"To tell her I love her, and help however I can."

Melody's glare melted into a look of compassion. "I'm sorry, Eric. Want me to see if I can get in touch with them for you?"

"Please. I need to know where I should head once I get to the city."

Melody gave him a hug, and he awkwardly patted her on the back. "I'll find a way. Don't worry. Get going."

"Happy to. I'll check in on the road. Stef said he'd be willing to take over at the Sullivan site until I get back."

"Good. We'll be okay. You go bring Libby back."

As Eric drove back to his house, he hoped like hell he'd be able to.

nineteen

Libby checked herself out in her bedroom mirror one last time. She smoothed down the skirt of the suit she wore and blew out a breath.

Mr. Billings had asked her to dress as staid as possible, and she couldn't think how much more staid she could get than a skirted navy suit, a cream silk blouse, taupe tights that she'd had to hunt down, and a pair of low navy heels. The chef's kiss touch was a pearl necklace that her Grandmother Hartwell had given her on her sixteenth birthday. She hadn't worn the necklace since her grandmother died five years ago, but it would be perfect for today.

If everything went as Mr. Billings hoped the court would toss her father from all trusts where she was a beneficiary, and likely bring him before the state bar association to have his license torn up.

"Libby? The car's waiting downstairs."

She straightened her shoulders and looked herself dead in the eye in the mirror. "You know your shit. No one can take your freedom from you." Then she turned and headed out of her bedroom to meet Michael.

When she'd headed back to New York from Sunflower

Falls, she'd never imagined that she'd need a bodyguard, but it had quickly become apparent that it was necessary. Eric's friend Zach had reached out after she'd told Eric about some unfortunate incidents with paparazzi, and he got her and Greer in touch with the firm he had been associated with when he'd lived in Los Angeles. Michael had shown up less than twenty-four hours later.

Michael smiled at her. "You ready?"

"As much as I'll ever be."

"Just remember to keep your head down and stick to my side like glue."

She nodded. She wished Mayzie was here to give her some good luck licks, but they'd taken her over to Greer's last night. No one wanted her dog on her own.

They got down to the lobby of the building, and Michael led the way out to the sedan. Thankfully, there were only a handful of paparazzi haunting her building. It was going to be worse down by the courthouse. The ones that had staked out her building quickly got on mopeds and followed the car down to the courthouse.

Just another thing to lie at her father's feet. She had never spoken with the press, except through Mr. Billings. But her father had held press conferences almost every week, laying the blame for all of this at her feet.

He was only a caring father, fearful of those who would take advantage of her. She couldn't be trusted to properly manage the money from the estate left to her by her maternal grandparents.

Libby hadn't even realized there was an estate left to her by them. She'd thought all the family money had come from the Hartwell side. She didn't remember her mom's parents as they'd died soon after her mother did.

Then there had been all the lurid photos splashed about in the press.

Honestly, whenever she'd looked at them, they reminded her of fun times with friends in college. Her father, though, had used them to paint her as an inveterate party girl. Only out for a good time.

As he'd infamously said in one interview. "Just look at her career choices. Managing so-called influencers."

She and Greer had immediately put out a statement about how proud they were to have been chosen to support the influencers they represented, and that Libby was taking a temporary leave of absence to deal with the legal issues involving her family to give the business and their clients a buffer.

Greer had spent half a day on the phone, talking with each of their clients, and shutting them down from going after her father. It had warmed her heart that all of their clients wanted to support her using their platforms, but as Greer had reminded them, her father still had some power, and saying anything directly about him could land them in a place they didn't want to be.

New York traffic was brutal as usual, but they eventually pulled up in front of the courthouse. Michael was on his phone. She listened with half an ear, familiar with the routine of him checking with Mr. Billings to ensure her father had already arrived and entered the courthouse.

He glanced over at her. "How much longer?" He frowned. "Fine. Call me when it's clear."

"What's going on?"

"Your father is hosting one of his press conferences."

Libby moved closer so she could look out the window. With as many people as were walking down the street, she didn't see what was going on at first. But she eventually saw him on the lower part of the steps leading up to the entrance of the courthouse. Her father was the epitome of the description "patrician lawyer". Dark suit, close-cut greying brown hair, his beard and mustache trimmed, and wire-rimmed glasses sitting on his nose. If you got close, you could make out the grey eyes that rarely held warmth. The only time she saw him smile was when he'd won in a way that completely trounced his opponent.

"What do we do?"

Michael gently eased her back to her seat. "Wait."

They had to wait fifteen minutes, and one of the security guards stopped by to see why they hadn't moved. When their driver explained who she was, the guard nodded and moved on.

Eventually, she and Michael made their way into the building and through to security, where they met up with Mr. Billings. He tried to reassure her that the court had noted her father's antics.

She let out a long breath. "As long as the judge won't penalize us for arriving late."

Mr. Billings pressed the up button for the elevator bank they needed. "I've already been in contact with the judge's clerk, and they are well aware of the reason for the delay. As your father had been warned about his press conferences, it did not go over well."

The elevator was packed with others headed up to the same floor they were, and they were last off. They made it into the courtroom assigned to their judge just as she was entering the room.

Mr. Billings immediately headed for his table and registered his appearance on her behalf.

When the judge inquired about her presence, she stood. The judge nodded, and the hearing began.

It was not pleasant. She wished she'd been able to have Greer here for support, but she'd been allowed only one non-party person, and both she and Mr. Billings agreed Michael was the best option. No one expected her father to do anything to her in court, but they needed to be prepared, just in case.

The judge called her father to the stand. After he was sworn in, his attorneys led him through his tired arguments of why she should be declared incapable of managing her life.

Toward the end of his testimony, he revealed he had been working to locate her after her disappearance from her wedding.

"All I cared about was her happiness after her groom left her at the altar. However, I was blocked from being assured of that by her business partner. That woman turned my daughter against me, and I believe she is holding my daughter captive through undue influence."

Libby had to bite her lips so as not to call him a lying liar in court. The judge would not be happy with that kind of outburst. Even if she likely agreed with it.

Her father continued working to paint himself as a loving and caring father, but under Mr. Billings' cross-examination, the portrait became holier than moth-infested sweater storage.

Her father couldn't answer basic questions such as when she'd graduated high school, and what her college major had been. Nor could he answer anything a caring father would be expected to know, such as when her birthday—October twenty-seventh—was or the name of her dog. Not that she'd told her father she'd gotten a dog. In fact, the distaste on his face and glare he sent in her direction when questioned about Mayzie certainly didn't help his testimony.

Finally, Mr. Billings closed out his cross-examination. Her father's attorneys presented what further evidence they could, and then it was her turn to testify.

She kept her gaze focused on Mr. Billings, or Michael

when she needed a neutral view, the entire time. She walked through her years growing up. The lack of care she received from her father. The changing of the nannies when they'd displeased him. Finally, she laid out the night before the wedding.

Mr. Billings smiled gently at her. "What did you discover when you returned to your apartment?"

She drew in a deep breath. "My father paid for my former apartment, but I believed that my former fiancè and I were the only ones with keys. I found out from the security guard that my father was up in the apartment, and that he'd been coming and going as he'd pleased the entire time I lived there."

"What else did you discover?"

"When I got to my apartment, I entered as quietly as possible. I didn't want a confrontation with either my father or my former fiancè. I heard them talking. They were in the living room, so I stayed behind a corner. I discovered my father was forcing my fiancè to marry me."

"Forcing your former fiancè how?"

Libby hadn't wanted to drag Herman and his family into this because it wasn't their fault that her father was a vindictive asshole. But Mr. Billings had coached her on answering directly, and without revealing too much about the details of their situation. Mainly because she couldn't confirm that they were true. "What I heard my father threaten my former fiancè with was the revelation of gambling debts his father held. I don't know if my former fiancè's father had or still has those gambling debts, just that was the threat my father made."

"And how did your former fiancè react?"

"He called my father a bastard."

"Did your father say anything in response?"

Libby took in a deep breath and let it out. Then another

one. She could still hear the coldness in her father's voice when he responded to Herman. "He said that he technically wasn't and therefore had the power to ensure Herman did what he wanted. And he wanted Herman to marry me the next morning, then keep me in line." She blinked, trying to keep her tears contained.

"What happened next, Ms. Hartwell?"

"I left. I could not go through with the wedding, and I called my maid of honor to inform her of that fact."

"Your maid of honor was Ms. Greer Branford, correct?"

"Yes."

"Does she fill any role in your life besides maid of honor?"

"She is also my business partner and my best friend."

"Did she ever try to talk you out of marrying your former fiancè?"

"Yes."

"Why do you suppose she did that?"

"I believe she was trying to be a good friend."

"Did she ever threaten your interest in your partnership or your friendship if you followed through with the marriage?"

"No."

They went through several questions designed to hobble her father's arguments that Greer was acting with undue influence over her. The judge asked some questions of her own before allowing her father's attorneys to question her.

They spent a grueling hour trying to tear her apart, but she refused to give her father any satisfaction. She knew she was winning when she spotted the one attorney grinding her teeth after answering a question regarding the number of times her father had assisted her in law school. The intimation that she would never have graduated if not for his help was clearly designed to rile her, but Mr. Billings had anticipated a question like this. Libby clearly laid out all the roadblocks her father put in place while she was in law school, and that she'd overcome.

The judge asked a few more follow-up questions regarding the business she and Greer were building. She gave examples of contracts she'd negotiated, as well as the names of some of their more publicly associated clients.

Her father's attorneys came back with a list of clients that had left their management and complained about them.

Mr. Billings then argued that every single one of those clients had left B&H for a firm that was run by a cousin of Libby's who had close ties to her father.

Finally, the judge closed the testimony portion of the day. She looked at each of the lead attorneys. "We are recessing for three hours. Please return to this courtroom at three. Mr. Hartwell, I strongly advise you to not speak with the press at all during this recess. I will not look upon such actions favorably."

His attorneys acknowledged the directive, and they all stood for the judge to exit. She and Mr. Billings waited until her father and his attorneys left, then they headed out.

Mr Billings arranged a couple of files in his briefcase before slipping the strap onto his shoulder. "Let's go to the cafeteria. I need to make some calls, but Michael can stay with you. I can guarantee that your father is unlikely to head there."

She and Michael made their way through the service line, and they found an unoccupied corner. Once Mr. Billings was assured she was settled, he headed off to do his other business. Michael handed her her phone.

"Thanks."

"You're welcome. Just so you know, I received a few

news alerts about you. Nothing huge, but maybe don't go looking." He looked uncomfortable. "Also, I had a message from Zach, but I haven't responded yet."

"From Zach?"

"Yeah. Some friend of yours is looking for you."

Libby immediately thought of Eric, but he knew she didn't want him here in town. Not while all this was going on and her father could discover who he was. "Thanks. Let me see if there're any messages."

She turned on and unlocked her phone. After it connected to the network, a slew of messages popped up from Greer and a few from Melody. There was even one from Eric. She went to the one from Eric first.

"I'm on my way. Tell me where to go."

Libby clapped her hand to her mouth. "Oh, no."

Michael's face immediately hardened as he looked around. "What?"

She waved her hand at him. "No. Not here. My friend, the one Zach must have messaged you about, is coming here."

Michael narrowed his eyes. "Do we need to do something about that?"

She shook her head, tears threatening once again. "No. It will be okay. I just...I just wasn't expecting him to come after I told him not to."

Michael immediately relaxed. "Oh. Well, if you change your mind. Let me know."

Libby laughed a little. "Thank you."

She wasn't sure how to respond to Eric, so she checked the messages from Melody and Greer. They each were warning her that Eric was on his way. Well, Melody's messages were also trying to find out where to direct her brother, as she didn't want him to overshoot and drive off into the East River. Greer wanted to know if Libby wanted her to run interference.

Greer knew the real reason Libby didn't want Eric in town. She didn't want him tainted by what her father was capable of.

Neither Greer nor Libby had expected the lengths her father would go to gain control of Libby. Not only had he filed for guardianship, but he had also filed a complaint against Greer with the state bar association, which she was currently fighting.

She had been so pissed off by the move that she filed a very detailed counterclaim. They had both agreed that the next step would be to sue her father for tortious interference. It wasn't a step they particularly wanted to take, but if he wanted to push things, they'd push right back.

And pushing back also included not being afraid to live her life the way she wanted to. She texted both Greer and Melody that she would get in contact with Eric. Since he might still be driving, she called him. Luckily, because they were in a corner, the background noise wasn't too bad.

The call rang a few times before Eric answered. "Finally decided to get in touch with me?"

She heard the smile in his tone and relaxed. "Well, Melody was worried you'd drive straight into the East River if you weren't told where to go."

Eric snorted. "I am not the person in our family who is that directionally challenged."

Libby bit her lips to hold in a laugh before replying. "You'll have to tell me that story sometime."

"You can hear it straight from Melody. So, where am I going?"

"You can go to my apartment. There's a parking garage down the block, and I'll let my doorman know to expect you." She gave him her address.

"Will you be waiting for me?"

Libby drew abstract lines on the table with her finger. "No. I'm at the courthouse. I don't know when I'll be done."

"You're not in court right now, right?"

It was Libby's turn to snort. "If I was making a phone call in a courtroom, you can bet you'd be hearing the judge yelling at me. No. We're in the cafeteria right now. The court is recessed until three."

"What happens then?"

She began tapping her finger against the table. "I don't know. Both my father and I testified today, basically presenting our cases about the need for guardianship. The one thing in my favor is that my attorney submitted a report from both my court-assigned guardian and two very reputable psychiatrists that it was unlikely that I needed to be placed under guardianship."

There was silence on Eric's end long enough that she wondered what was going on. She was about to ask if he was okay when he asked a question. "Why all of this, then? Couldn't they just submit the reports and have the case thrown out?"

She sighed. "No. Even when it becomes clear there isn't any cause for guardianship, the court has to go through the process after they've allowed it to move forward. We'll see what the judge says."

Michael tapped the table in front of her. She frowned at him. "Hold on, Eric." She placed her hand over the microphone. "What?"

He held up his phone. "Just got a message from Mr. Billings. Court is resuming in fifteen minutes."

Not bothering to argue, Libby held the phone back up to her mouth. "Eric, I'm sorry. I've got to go. I'll call my building and let them know you're coming." She hung up before he could say anything else and made the authorization call to her building's concierge desk.

Then she and Michael hurried back to the courtroom. Mr. Billings met them at the door, and they all entered the courtroom. One of her father's attorneys was standing at the table, but the other attorney and her father were missing. The judge was settling herself in her chair.

She waved at them and her father's attorney. "Counsel, please approach the bench."

Libby sat with Michael while the attorneys and judge discussed whatever had happened. When the attorneys headed back to the respective tables, Mr. Billings gestured for Libby to join him.

Confused, she headed to the seat next to him. The judge looked at all of them in turn and then made her pronouncement. "This court finds in favor of Miss Liberty Hartwell and dismisses the filing for guardianship over her with prejudice. Court dismissed."

Libby looked at Mr. Billings, shocked. "What happened?"

He smiled at her. "You're a free woman, Liberty." His smile turned into a grin. "Your father, however, is not."

twenty

Eric looked up as the door to the apartment building's lobby opened. Just as he had the last twenty times the door had opened.

He ran over when he saw it was finally Libby. He picked her up and swung her around. And then caught the glare of the guy who'd been identified as her bodyguard in the press.

"You okay, Libby?"

Eric wanted to growl at the familiar tone to the guy's words, but Libby patted him on the chest before turning around. He didn't want to let her go, but he also didn't want to get into a fight with the guy. Not only because he knew he'd lose.

"I'm fine, Michael. This is Eric. You can go off duty for now. We're just going to head to my apartment."

"If you want to go out, even with him, call me. You're going to be inundated with the press with the news."

"News?" Eric pulled Libby back into his arms.

She looked up at him over her shoulder. "I'll tell you when we're in my apartment. I need to get out of these clothes and eat something."

"I'll stay here in the lobby just in case anyone tries to get past the doorman. Let me know if you decide to order anything, and I'll handle it."

Libby grinned at the guy. "Thank you, Michael."

She tugged on Eric's hand. "Come on. Where are your bags?"

"Just brought the one." He detoured back to the chair he'd been sitting in and grabbed his bag from the floor.

Libby led him to the elevators, and they stayed silent as one of her neighbors got on behind them with a small black dog who was territorial about its space.

"Hey, Libby. Where's Mayzie?" Her neighbor was relaxed, but held their dog's leash in a tight grip.

"She's hanging out with a friend. I know she's probably missing Titus."

Her neighbor laughed and then picked up the dog—who started growling—when the elevator dinged for their floor. "Like anyone but me misses Titus. Have a good one."

They got off without the dog doing anything worse than growling, and Libby led him down the hall and around the corner from the elevator. Her apartment was at the end of the hall, in a corner of the building. She pulled out her keys and unlocked the door.

His first impression was that she had decent lighting from all the windows. Even if the space between the side set and the building next door was probably no more than five feet. The apartment was decently sized, with a nicely laid out living space that flowed into a galley kitchen.

She didn't have much in the way of furniture, however. A couch, a TV stand, and the TV was all that was in the living space. The kitchen also seemed like Libby didn't put it to its full use. When he and Libby had regularly started sleeping together, she'd cook the odd meal, but mostly, he had been the one to cook.

"When did you move in?"

She headed down a hall that led past the kitchen. "About a month ago? I stayed with Greer for the first couple of weeks. But we both realized that I needed my own space."

"How far away is Greer's place?" He could hear her rustling around, and imagined her stripping down. His dick started responding, and he had to force the thoughts from his brain as he did not want her coming back in the room and find him sporting a full woody.

Libby laughed. "Next block over." She came out of the bedroom dressed in leggings and a loose t-shirt. "I'm ready to celebrate."

"Sure. What exactly are we celebrating?"

She came over, cupped his face, and pulled him down to meet her kiss. It was deep and long. He placed his hands on her hips. She moved one hand to his and repositioned his hand on her ass. He took the hint and pulled her in close. It felt so good to feel her body pressed up against his again.

When they came up for air, she grinned at him. "First, we're celebrating that you're here. Even though I told you I didn't want you to come here."

He winced. "I'm sorry."

She cuddled into his chest. "This time only, don't be. I wish you'd been here earlier, but I'm so glad my father didn't find out about you."

Eric worried she'd want to keep him as her dirty little secret. But then he realized she hadn't kept their relationship a secret from Greer at all. She may not want to introduce him to her father, but she had no problems with her best friend knowing about him. "What else are we celebrating?"

"Have you looked at the news at all?"

"No. I didn't get here much before you, and I spent most of the time talking with your building's concierge."

"Lalitha's a sweetheart. I have a feeling she's going to be celebrating the news, too, even though it'll likely mean more paparazzi hanging around the building."

He put his finger under her chin and tipped her face up so he could see her better. "What. News?"

Libby grinned. "My father got arrested today."

"What?"

"It turns out that back when Herman left town..."

"Wait, who is Herman?"

She winced. "My ex."

It was his turn to wince. "Is it bad that I feel sorry for the guy, if only because his parents decided Herman was a good choice of name?"

"Well, he went by pretty much anything but Herman. Anyway, before he left town with his secretary, he also submitted a bunch of documents to the FBI and the state attorney general that documented years of my father's misappropriating funds from client escrow accounts."

Eric frowned. "I get from the fact that he submitted them to the FBI and attorney general's office that it's not good, but how does that mean your father gets arrested?"

"Let's sit down."

He moved them to the couch and tucked her under his arm. "Are you going to need a whiteboard to explain this to me?"

"Hopefully not. Embezzling from client escrow accounts is pretty much the worst thing you can do as an attorney."

"Ah. Like signing off on a home inspection knowing that the foundation is compromised and needs significant repairs."

Libby shrugged. "Probably. Anyway, the AG's office has

been investigating my father since I ran from my wedding. He hasn't helped matters with this case, as it became clear he had also hidden and embezzled funds that I was entitled to."

Eric hugged her. "I'm sorry."

She let out a long sigh. "I'm...ambivalent at this point. Like, I don't know that I expected anything better from him after finding out that he was trying to force my marriage to someone he could control."

They were silent for a bit as they each digested what that meant for Libby. He hugged her again. "Want me to make something for dinner?"

She shook her head. "I don't really have much in the fridge. At least, not anything to make a complete meal for the both of us."

He thought that over. "Get delivery a lot, do you?"

She pinched him. "What else is living in the city good for if not having delivery available at all hours of the day?"

"Fine. Remind me of one of the drawbacks of Sunflower Falls."

She lifted her head and pressed a kiss against his jaw. "No delivery, but you're an excellent cook and you keep your kitchen reasonably stocked."

He pressed a kiss against her lips. "At least I know why you value me."

She ran her hand down his chest and into his pants. His dick stirred again as he felt her fingers undo the button and zipper on his jeans. "I value more than your cooking skills."

He shifted, so that he was laying down on the couch, and she was draped over him. "Glad to know that, too."

They kissed and slowly undressed each other until the only thing he was wearing were his boxers. Libby was completely naked. The feel of her skin under his hands was what he'd been craving for weeks. But the couch was not the place he wanted to be for this reunion.

"Bedroom?"

Her breathing was heavier than normal as she pressed a kiss against his pec. "Sure."

He got his feet on the floor and got up. Then he lifted her into his arms. She giggled, and the sheer joy of the sound had him feeling like he could conquer anything. Her bedroom had a bit more going on than in the living room, but not much more.

The clothes she'd been wearing when she came home were tossed onto a chair in a corner. Her bed was covered in a cream-colored bedspread, and the pillows were neatly stacked against a basic headboard.

He set her down slowly so that every part of her body stroked against his. She cupped the back of his head and pulled down. He kissed her, stroking his tongue in and out. Libby responded by hooking her leg up against his thigh, pressing her pelvis hard against his.

"Wait. I've got to grab a condom from my bag."

"Don't worry. I've got some in the nightstand drawer."

He leaned back. "You weren't expecting me in town. Why do you have condoms in the nightstand drawer?" He winced as he realized what he'd just said was an an asshole move. "Don't answer that. I'm sorry."

She nipped his lip with her teeth. "Relax. It was habit more than anything else." She turned around and stripped the bed before climbing up onto it. She curled a finger at him. "Come here."

He laughed. "Fine. You've got condoms. What about the lube?"

She lifted a brow. "I didn't have you, but I still had my toys. Of course I've got lube."

Eric placed one knee on the bed and cupped her shoulder. He leaned down and pressed kisses on her skin, starting with her other shoulder, across her collarbone and neck to her jaw.

"Eric."

He pressed a kiss against the corner of her mouth. "Libby."

She reached up and tangled her fingers in her hair, pulling him down on top of her. He shucked his boxers and relished the feel of being completely skin to skin with her again.

He shifted his legs so that one thigh slid between hers, her already damp core rubbing against him.

"Eric?"

"Yeah?" He moved down and sucked one nipple into his mouth.

She groaned and rubbed harder against his thigh. He wondered if they'd need lube this round. But he'd still use it because he'd rather her not be sore when they could have used it.

"I need you in me. Now."

He lifted his head and saw the determination on her face. Looking over, he spotted the night stand. It took a bit of fumbling, but he eventually got the drawer open and the lube and a strip of condoms onto the bed. He poured some lube into his hand and worked it into her pussy.

Libby gripped his wrist, holding him tight to her. Shudders shook her body, and he realized she'd been closer to orgasm than he realized. "Damn."

A blissed out expression covered her face as she opened her eyes. "It's been too long."

He quickly sheathed himself with the condom and then shifted his body so he could press inside of her. Once he was fully seated in her, and trying not to come as her inner muscles contracted around him, he caged her upper body with his arms and kissed her.

Eric held as still as possible as he wanted—needed—this full connection with Libby. She must have understood, as she wrapped her arms up behind his shoulders and hooked her thighs around his hips.

Coming up for air, he looked at her. Brushed a lock of hair away from her face. "I don't want to leave you here."

She smiled up at him. "I'm not letting you go back alone."

"Don't you need to stay here?"

"You really know how to pick the mid-sex conversation." She hugged him with her whole body. "I doubt it. Maybe a couple of days? Just to pack. If I need to come back for anything, I can drive."

He began shifting in her, nothing frantic as he wanted to extend this moment of peace as long as possible. "Do you even have a car?"

She laughed. "Not yet. I figured you can take me car shopping back home."

"Home?"

She placed her hand over his heart. "Yeah. New York's never really been my home. I only realized that after I came back here. I want to be with you in Sunflower Falls."

He dropped his head so his forehead met hers. "Thank, Christ. If you'd wanted me to move here, I would have found a way, but…"

She arched her hips up, and he began moving faster. "Yeah, but. We've got time later to talk about this. In detail. Fuck me now."

Unable to deny her, he began moving even faster, pushing up on his arms to change the angle of his thrusts. When it looked like she was getting even closer, he reached down and made a circling motion on her clit.

Her hips bucked, almost throwing him off. "Come on, Libby. Come for me."

She never took her gaze off his as she came. She was the most beautiful being in the world. And she was coming home with him. Unable to hold back any longer, he let his orgasm rush through his body.

The pleasure sapped all his energy as it ebbed away. He disengaged from her and flopped over onto his side. Neither of them were breathing with any kind of rhythm. Finally, she turned over and faced him.

Her smile reminded him of morning sunrise hitting the lake while out fishing with Uncle Stef. Glowing and full of promise.

"Hi."

"Hi."

She threaded her fingers into his hair behind his ear. "I'm glad you're here."

He moved in and kissed her lightly. "I'm glad I came. I love you." He hadn't planned on saying that, but it felt so right and true to the moment.

If her previous smile was morning sunrise, her grin was the noon sun in June. "I love you, too." She blew out a long breath. "I didn't know that I'd ever be able to say that."

He wrapped his arms around her and hugged her. "You don't know how much I needed to hear that."

"Worried while driving eight hours to see me?"

He laughed. "Maybe. I would have been here earlier, but I hit traffic."

She pulled his earlobe. "It is a rare day that there isn't traffic."

Eric shifted onto his back and pulled her up over him. "I managed it once. Just before seven in the morning on a Sunday."

"Now you're just bragging." She crossed her arms on his chest and rested her chin on them.

The angle wasn't the best, but he tried to hold her gaze. "It's not bragging if it's true."

"You're really okay with me coming back to Sunflower Falls?"

"Babe, I was not kidding that I'd figure out a way to stay if you needed me here. I'd rather be with you than without you. But the crew's been giving me grief, asking when you'd be back."

"And you're okay with Mayzie coming with me?"

"I'm more than okay with you being a package deal. If I hadn't made it clear, I like your dog. And I'm pretty sure she likes me, too."

"That's because you feed her from the table. Which I've learned is not a good thing."

"We'll negotiate."

She laughed and pushed up. "Go get cleaned up."

"Time for dinner?"

"Yep. I'm going to take a quick shower when you're done…"

He jacked up out of bed and then picked her up. She squealed, but wrapped her arms around his neck. "Great idea. We'll shower together."

She kissed him, and he kissed her back. "Are you always going to be like this?"

"Until I can't carry you anymore, and even then, I'll just prop you up on my walker."

She laid her head on his shoulder. "Sweet talker."

"For you? Always. Let's go start the rest of our lives."

epilogue

MELODY FOUND A PLACE TO PARK HER TRUCK ON THE SHOULDER OF the road. The annual fundraiser for the volunteer fire department looked like it was going to be another success.

Harry had blocked off Geraghty's parking lot so grills, games, and vendor booths could be set up, which meant half the town had parked up and down the road. As she was walking up the road, she spotted Eric's truck. She did a little shimmy as she passed it.

When she'd dropped Button off with her mom and found Mayzie already there, she wasn't sure if Eric and Libby were on their way here or were taking advantage of the excuse to get some private time to themselves.

There was still a bit of a crowd standing at the parking lot's entrance, so she prepped herself for small talk. It wasn't like her neighbors and friends annoyed her, but she was more interested in getting one-on-one time with one particular person.

"Hello, Melody."

And that person was not Mrs. Smith. Melody plastered a smile across her face and walked up to the older lady. "Hi, Mrs. Smith. How are you doing?"

"Fine. It's a lovely day, isn't it?"

"It is. Are you hosting a booth this year?"

"Yes. Be sure to stop by. I have something you might be particularly interested in."

When Mrs. Smith thought Melody would be particularly interested in something, she was almost a hundred percent correct. "I will."

They shuffled closer to the tables where some of the volunteer firefighters were taking the entrance fees. "I saw that nice Tony Caputo here earlier when I was setting up the booth. He was helping Zach Troy."

Melody ground her teeth. "I'm sure he was."

If Tony Caputo wasn't hovering over her at the site of his new home, he was out doing something with Zach. She'd never gotten a clear explanation from either of them about why they spent so much time together. They were friends, yeah, and definitely weren't anything more than friends. But Zach wasn't working now, and Tony obviously had money to do things like take a surprise trip over to Niagara and buy a home to do a tear-down and rebuild on the lot.

"I thought I saw your brother's truck. Are he and Libby here?"

"I think so. I doubt either would have come without the other."

"How is she doing? I read her father had bond denied at his arraignment hearing."

Melody shrugged. "Fine, I guess. We don't really talk about that when I see them." In fact, Libby had declared that all discussion of her father to be a forbidden topic unless she brought it up. Melody had gotten the impression that Libby was waiting to see what came out at the hearing.

When she'd made that suggestion to Ana, Ana had just

replied that she wished her own mother had done something so egregious that she'd get arrested.

Not that Melody had room to talk, considering her own father. The asshole had the gall to show up and demand money from her earlier in the summer. She'd threatened to turn him into the cops as she'd been keeping track of him and had come across a few open warrants.

They got up to the entrance tables, and Andy Kavanaugh smiled up at them. "Hello, ladies. That will be five bucks each, please."

As Mrs. Smith opened her purse, Melody grabbed her wallet from her pocket. "I've got this. How are you doing, Andy?" She pulled out a ten and handed it to him.

"Good." He put it in the canvas pouch. "Hey, just a head's up that Alex is going to be coming back to town next week."

Her teenaged heart let out a happy sigh. "Oh, really? Is he planning on sticking around?"

"Not sure, but I thought you might like a head's up."

"Thanks."

Andy had been in her class, and Alex had been in Zach's, a year ahead of Eric. It had been kind of funny. Zach had been the bad boy star football player who looked like Mr. All-American, while Alex had been the town golden boy hockey star who looked like he could have been on the popular teen vampire show playing at the time.

Then Zach had signed up for the Marines and become a decorated hero, while Alex had gotten drafted into the NHL and had built a reputation of a guy not to mess with.

Mrs. Smith hooked her arm into Melody's, derailing that trip down memory lane. "Thank you very much for the entrance fee. Come over to my booth so I can show you what I found."

Considering Mrs. Smith's grip was very strong for someone she knew to be older than her mother, Melody followed along.

The item Mrs. Smith had set aside for her was a lovely wooden box with a marquetry design on the top. "It's a puzzle box, but I knew you'd love it as soon as I came across it."

Melody lightly stroked the top. "Oh, thank you. It's gorgeous. Where did you find it?"

"In a lovely little thrift shop up in Montreal when I took that buying trip last month."

"How much?"

"One hundred dollars."

Melody looked up. "One hundred? Really, Mrs. Smith?" She was gearing up to negotiate like they did every time Mrs. Smith found a treasure like this for her, when she felt a presence behind her, and shivered.

"She'll take it."

Tony Caputo was so close behind her she couldn't whirl around and glare at him, but she certainly felt the movement of his body as he did something, then reached around her with a hundred-dollar bill held out to Mrs. Smith.

The woman grinned at him as she plucked the bill from his hand. "Nice doing business with you."

When he did finally give her enough space, Melody turned to ream him out, but he was already walking away. He winked at her over his shoulder. "Keep your special things inside of it."

She couldn't say anything without drawing unwanted attention, so she let out a muffled shriek—because she had to do something—before turning back to Mrs. Smith. She held out the puzzle box. "Can you hold on to this for me? I'll be back when I'm ready to leave."

"Of course."

Before Mrs. Smith could say anything further, she headed after Caputo. She didn't see him in the crowd hanging out in the parking lot, so she headed inside of Geraghty's. There was a pool tournament scheduled, so maybe he was in there to watch.

She spotted Libby and Eric hanging out by the bar, so went over to say hi.

Libby gave her a hug, and Eric fist bumped her. "How's it going?"

"Good. Did either of you see Tony Caputo come in? I need to yell at him."

Libby held up a hand to hide what Melody was sure was a grin, and Eric shook his head. "What happened now? Something with the house?"

"No. He paid for something I was going to buy from Mrs. Smith."

Libby's eyes widened. "He bought it out from under you?"

"No. He bought it for me, but he paid full price for it."

Eric paused in the middle of picking up his pint of beer. "So, why is this a problem?"

"First, he bought it for me without asking. Second, part of the fun with buying stuff from Mrs. Smith is haggling with her, and I didn't get to do that."

Eric rolled his eyes. "Only you would be mad at someone buying something for you because it blocked you from being able to haggle."

"Stop being mean to her."

"I'm her big brother. I'm allowed to be mean."

Melody held up her hands. "Before this devolves into a lover's spat, did either of you see him?"

Eric jerked his thumb over his shoulder in the direction of the pool tables. "He headed that way."

She patted him on the shoulder. "Thanks."

She worked her way through the crowd, stopping to talk with a few people who wouldn't let her pass otherwise before she made it to the edge of the pool table area. She spotted his head of brownish hair as he was turning and moving around the group gathered closest to the tables.

Melody growled as she realized he was escaping her again. He had a clearer exit, as she had to go back through the crowd.

Finally, she made it over to the entrance to the kitchen, where she'd last seen him. She poked her head inside and saw Harry's latest head cook manning the deep fryer. "Did you see Tony Caputo?"

The man nodded over to where the back entrance of the building was.

"Thanks." When she got to the door, she realized it hadn't fully closed and she could hear Tony talking to someone.

She inched the door open and tried to look out without making herself obvious. Tony flashed past her, and she realized he was on the phone, not paying any attention to what was going on around him.

Turning her head, she tried to listen in.

"I know that wasn't the plan. But it's the plan now."

He was quiet for a few beats, and she could hear someone else talking. Likely whoever was on the other end of the call. And they didn't sound like they were happy.

"Stop. Either this gets registered under my legal name, or I'm backing out. I'll blow your whole project up, and I'll make it known why I'm doing it."

Melody slapped her hand over her mouth so he wouldn't hear her gasp. His legal name? Why the hell was he threatening to blow up some project if something didn't happen with his legal name?

Her heart felt like it was about to break into pieces, but she had to stay quiet and listen to what else he had to say. She realized he'd started talking again, so she worked to focus on his words instead of the fear that was building inside of her.

"Listen. No one here knows who I really am. I've kept my head low, like you told me to. But this needs to end. Soon. Do what I say."

Melody blinked back tears as she shoved the door open. Tony whirled around as metal scraped against concrete.

Shock filled his face, but he replied to the person on the other end of the line. "I've got to go." He pressed the screen of his phone and stared at her. "Melody..."

She held up a hand even as she shook her head. Tears flew off her face. "I don't want to hear it. In fact, I don't want to hear anything more from you." She swallowed the sob that threatened to erupt and forced the words she needed to say out. "I want a divorce."

***

Want a peek at Libby and Eric's wedding? Register for my newsletter here:

By signing up for my newsletter, you'll also be among the first to find out news of the shenanigans brewing between Melody and Tony!

about the author

Katie Lillig is a long-time romance reader, published previously under a different pen name, and loves playing with office supplies.

Website & newsletter: katielillig.com

facebook.com/authorkatielillig
instagram.com/katielillig
tiktok.com/@katielillig